Secret of
the Dance

Secret of the Dance

A Novel By

Susan Eileen Walker

Keene Publishing
Warwick, New York

KEENE
PUBLISHING
P. O. Box 54
Warwick, New York 10990
www.KeeneBooks.com

Library of Congress Cataloging-in-Publication Data

Walker, Susan Eileen, 1962-
  Secret of the dance : a novel / by Susan E. Walker.— 1st ed.
    p. cm.
  ISBN -10: 0-9766805-4-8
  ISBN-13: 978-0-9766805-4-3
  1. Dance—Fiction. 2. Teenage—Fiction.
  3. Relationships—Fiction. 4. Ballet—Fiction.
  I. Title.

PS3611.U25N45 2006
813'.6—dc22   2006007232

Printed in the United States of America.

10 9 8 7 6 5 4 3 2 1

For Tom, my son who wanted his name in a book and for Blonnie Bunn Wyche, thank you for the inspiration.
—S. E. W.

Dance is the hidden language of the soul.

—Martha Graham,
 U.S. choreographer and dancer (1893 - 1991)

1

*R*emi Applewhite looked from the envelope to her father. This was it, the letter she'd been waiting two months for. The one that could make her dreams a reality or crush them to dust. All she had to do was open the envelope and read the contents. At sixteen, she was sometimes strong and outgoing, but other times—like now—she was shy and fearful of everything.

"I can't open this. You do it, Daddy," she said, holding the letter out.

"Show some backbone, girl. You're an Applewhite, not a scaredy cat," her great-grandmother, Dottie, said from the other side of the table. "Hurry up and open it while the pie is still warm."

"Yes, ma'am." Remi opened the envelope and pulled out a single page. Unfolding it, she read aloud. "Dear Miss Applewhite. Thank you for your interest in LaGuardia High School. At this time we are not taking applications from outside the New York City school district. If you were to relocate to the area, we would be happy to take a second look at your application and audition video. You also need to concentrate on gaining more production experience."

"Well, that sucks," Dottie said, breaking the silence. She cut Remi's wedge of apple pie twice the normal size and expertly served it to a plate.

"Dottie!"

Both Remi and her father, Chance, protested the old woman's language.

Dottie looked from one to the other. "What? Did you think I didn't know the word? I'm old, not out of touch. So what are you going to do now? Are you sure you want to go to this school?"

"This is a wonderful school and has a great training program for dancers," Remi said, wiping away tears of disappointment.

"So what are you going to do now?" Dottie asked, handing Chance his slice of pie and cutting a small wedge for herself.

Weekly dinner with Dottie and her father always challenged Remi. Dottie demanded real conversation, opinions, thoughts, and debate in full sentences. She did not allow single word answers, grunts, or animal sounds that might suffice elsewhere.

Remi took a bite of pie and savored it while trying to come up with other options than giving up on her dream. "I can't think of anything. I guess I could always call Uncle Jeremy and beg him to let me live with him so I qualify for school."

"No! Absolutely not!" Chance yelled as he jumped out of his chair. He stared at her as if she'd just vowed to burn down the school in protest.

"Sit down, Chance," Dottie said.

Remi stared at her father, her heart pounding at his violent reaction to what seemed like the perfect solution. "But Dad, he lives in New York City. I could live with him, go to school, and maybe get a job as a real dancer."

Chance sat down and took several deep breaths before speaking. Whenever he did this, Remi knew he was trying to get himself under control. Finally he said, "Jeremy's a stranger. He's been gone for seventeen years and hasn't bothered to contact us once. You will not call him out of the blue and ask to live with him. You'll just have to come up with another solution."

"But Daddy…"

"No child, leave him be. Jeremy might be family, but we don't know what he's like these days." Dottie patted Remi's arm. "We'll just have to come up with another way to get you into that school. Now you dry the dishes while your father washes." Dottie gave out the clean up assignments, then settled back with her coffee cup.

"Yes, ma'am," Remi said. She returned the letter to its envelope, then rose to carry her dishes to the sink.

Half an hour later a horn sounded. "Mom's here," Remi said as she gathered her belongings. She hugged her father, then her great-grandmother. "I'll see you next week, Dottie," she said.

"Instead of calling, it might be better to write a letter," Dottie whispered as she pressed a folded piece of paper into Remi's hand. "I love you, child."

"I love you, too," Remi said, not understanding, but closing her fist around the paper anyway.

Once she was in the car, Remi turned on the map light and unfolded the piece of yellow paper. Then it all became clear. Instead of calling her uncle, Dottie had suggested she write him a letter. Remi thought about it all the way home and decided that her great-grandmother was right. That way she could think everything through and make her argument in just the right way. She also wouldn't get flustered like she would if she talked to her world famous uncle on the phone.

❧

"Dottie, why don't we call you Grandma?" Remi asked the following Saturday. She was helping to peel the many apples it would take to make enough applesauce to fill the twenty-four pint jars sitting on the counter. To Dottie, fall meant days of work canning and pickling and filling her basement pantry for the year ahead. She preferred to do it herself because that way she knew that each jar was filled with fresh ingredients in the proper amounts.

Dottie paused in cutting an apple for the cooking pot. "That's an interesting question. I guess it all started with your Grandma Cathryn. She tried to teach your daddy and Uncle Jeremy to call me Grandmama. None of us liked it. The boys had a hard time pronouncing it, and I thought it sounded high faluting. I preferred Granny or Nana, but your grandma insisted, and no one could tell her any different.

"When the boys came to live with me, Chance was thirteen and refused to call me Grandmama. Jeremy was eleven and followed his brother's lead. I didn't care what they called me, so we all agreed to Dottie. When you were born, I guess we didn't think of having you call me any different."

"Did you write to your uncle?" Dottie asked, changing the subject.

"Yes, ma'am. I mailed it out yesterday," Remi said.

"Good for you. Let's hope he reads it and doesn't have some assistant send you an autographed picture."

They continued working, mostly in silence, but occasionally Remi would throw out a story request and Dottie was happy to oblige. Finally the old woman looked at the girl and said, "You are beautiful, child. Don't let anyone tell you any different. You have the look of your father about you."

"Really? Everyone always tells me I look like Mom," Remi said, finishing one apple and reaching for another.

"Oh, you look like Stacy, but I see your father in you, especially about the eyes."

By the time the applesauce was cooked and put up, Dottie was looking pale. "Are you all right?" Remi asked as they finished cleaning the kitchen.

Dottie paused in wiping off the table and frowned. "No, child, I don't think I am. Could you call your father? I don't think…" her words stuttered to a halt and she collapsed.

"Dottie!" Remi cried. She ran for the phone and dialed her father's cell number. She stretched the phone cord out so she could reach Dottie's side. "Come on, answer the phone. Daddy? Something's wrong with Dottie. She collapsed a minute ago and isn't waking up. Uh-huh, okay, bye."

Remi hung up the phone, then sank to her knees beside Dottie's body. Several long moments later, she finally heard the sirens as the ambulance came from the fire station a mile away. Dottie was still breathing, but she wasn't moving and had not opened her eyes or even moaned.

"Come on, Dottie. You can't die yet. You've got a million more stories to tell me about dancing and my dad and Uncle Jeremy. You can't die." Remi brushed at Dottie's white pin curls.

When the blaring sirens faded, Remi went to the back door. Her father followed the ambulance crew into the kitchen. "You okay?" he asked as he hugged her.

"I'm fine, but she's not," Remi said. She buried her face into her father's shoulder. Remi was thankful that he didn't say anything else. There wasn't anything to say.

In minutes Dottie was securely strapped to the stretcher, wheeled to the ambulance, and was on her way to the hospi-

tal in Winchester, Virginia, a fifty-mile drive on narrow, winding mountain roads. Remi and Chance followed after stopping at the dance school to tell Stacy the news. Dottie was
old and had lived a full life.

2

The beacon of headlights shone on the billboard in the curve of the road. This was the sign he'd been looking for, but it was much different than the last time he'd been to town.

Welcome to Romney, West Virginia, home of Jeremy Applewhite, Broadway Superstar. Population 2537.

Jeremy's foot slipped off the gas pedal as he read the sign. He stomped on the brakes as he angled over to the narrow shoulder and threw the gearshift into neutral. So they finally recognize me as something other than one of Dottie's crazy dancing grandsons, Jeremy thought. Too bad they'll have to change the sign from Broadway Superstar to broken down has-been.

Putting the car back into gear, he returned to the road and drove on. Romney had changed little since his last visit a decade and a half before. The only restaurant in town that served alcohol had changed its name. The grocery store was now a drug store. But the houses lining Main Street hadn't changed. They were still painted white with red doors and black shutters. The brick buildings still sported white trim and green doors.

The new traffic light in front of the school caught him by surprise. The town had grown enough to warrant more than the one light in front of the courthouse. The Civil War soldier still stood guard in front of the two-story county seat and courthouse, stalwartly guarding the intersection where

Highway 50 and Highway 29 came together.

Jeremy drove on, keeping the powerful car to twenty-four miles an hour. Whoever the nighttime deputy was would stop a speeder, even if he were only over the speed limit by a mile or two. That would give him bragging rights for a week at Harry's Barbershop. As he remembered, the town had closed up for the night. There were no other cars in sight. Only the dim streetlights and his car's headlights broke the early morning darkness.

The cemetery was, as always, still and dark. The sight of that long brick fence sent a cold chill through him, as it had every time he'd passed it since moving to town at the age of eleven. But that fence was the landmark he was looking for. Five more driveways before Dottie's. Surprising himself, he named the owners of those driveways.

"The Millers, the Saxtons, the Maxwells, Reverend Allbright, the Smiths."

Dottie's driveway was still gravel with grass poking through between the loose rocks. It curved away from the house toward the garage. He'd see about paving the drive as soon as he was settled in. He didn't glance toward the house. He didn't have to. Dottie hadn't changed the six-room clapboard house in all the years he'd lived there, why would it be different now? There would be mums on the front porch steps. The garden in back would be empty, covered over with leaves and waiting for spring planting.

At two-thirty in the morning, the house itself would be dark. It would remain dark for a couple more hours. Dottie would rise at daybreak for an hour of Bible study and prayer. That had been her habit for as long as Jeremy could remember, and he doubted she'd alter that hour of meditation, even if there was a strange car in her driveway.

Jeremy eased the car to a stop in front of the garage door. After turning off the engine, he stretched as best he could. But the movement did little to ease the tension and stiffness in his back, neck, and shoulders. Laying his head back, he closed his eyes and relaxed for the first time since leaving New York. He'd done it. He'd come home to the place he'd once vowed never to visit again because of the bitter feelings toward small towns and smaller minds. But here he was, for better or worse. Home to lick his wounds and figure out what to do with the next fifty or sixty years of his life.

He would climb out and stretch, but that would set off the neighborhood dogs. And the barking would wake Dottie. When he and Chance had tried to sneak in late, she had met them at the kitchen door. She never said a word. She had just stood there, arms crossed over her chest and a disappointed expression on her face.

Jeremy shifted to lay across the bench seat, stretching his five-foot-ten-inch frame as much as the car would allow. Stuffing the small pillow from the back seat between his head and the door, he tried to relax. Coming home shouldn't be this stressful.

Silence and the scattered blinking of lightning bugs filled the long summer evening. He'd missed that in New York. For the last seventeen years, he'd spent the occasional evening that he wasn't working at parties or out being seen by the paparazzi. His manager constantly reminded him that it was vital to be seen. He had to advertise himself, his current production, and his future one.

Jeremy shifted until he found a comfortable position. In three heartbeats, exhaustion dragged him into unconsciousness.

❧

Dreams do come true, Chance Applewhite thought. He crossed the wide stage, his feet flying through the complicated series of steps. His shaggy black-brown hair followed him like a flag as he threw himself into the air to fly for endless seconds. It felt as if he were suspended by wire four feet above the stage.

Michael Jordan, eat your heart out, he thought, landing on one foot before spinning and heading across the stage in a series of dizzying spins. Chance made the impossible moves look easy. His midnight blue costume set off his azure blue eyes, turning them silver to those in the front rows. The standing-room-only crowd gasped as he threw himself into the performance. How did such a large, bear-like man move through the dance with such grace?

Finally, the music died away. A stunned silence hung over the room before the applause began. Exhilarated and exhausted, Chance shifted to face the audience as a thunderous applause swelled. He bowed, noticing a run in his leotard. Rising for a moment, he bent into a second bow. This time, his costume was gone, blue-white jeans in its place. His dance shoes were gone as well, and he wore cowboy boots made from the rattlesnakes he'd caught as a young man.

A shrill beeping noise drowned out the applause. Jeremy was the dancer in the family. He owned a dance studio and a restaurant with a postage stamp-size dance floor in the corner.

The alarm continued its shrill beeping until Chance reached out and slapped the thing. With a groan that started in his toes, he rolled onto his back. He flung his arms wide across the double bed. He felt every one of his forty years.

He felt sore inside and out, as if he'd actually danced the intricate steps of his dream.

Even now, he could retrace the steps in his mind, seeing another dancer making the moves. The dance would be perfect for Remi, the studio's prize pupil and his sixteen-year-old daughter.

Climbing out of bed, Chance didn't bother pulling on clothes before heading to his desk. He began scribbling notes no one else could read. He was afraid he would forget the steps unless he committed them to paper right away.

Only when he'd jotted down the entire sequence as well as notes on the music did he finally look up. There was a silver car in the driveway. But it was no one local. No one in Romney drove such a car. That car cost more than he'd earned last year. Nope, this wasn't one of Dottie's friends. This was someone unexpected, but Chance didn't dare to hope that his brother had gotten any of the dozens of messages he'd left all over New York City. It was probably some yuppie lost in the mountains of West Virginia who'd pulled in for a couple of hours of sleep. It had happened before and no doubt it would happen again. Some people just didn't understand that the no trespassing sign posted by the driveway meant keep out.

Chance grabbed the jeans that were flung over a chair and pulled them up over bare skin. He shoved his feet into worn-out sneakers and picked up the aluminum baseball bat by the door. Then he made his way through the silent house and out the kitchen door. Whoever had shown up unannounced was about to get a rude introduction to dawn.

3

$\mathcal{J}$eremy tried to find a more comfortable position, but the pillow had shifted out from under his head. Twisting, he mashed his ear into the door's armrest. His left calf knotted into a pain-filled charley horse. Crying out, he shoved himself higher on the car door. He straightened his leg and tried to work out the cramp. With his knee still bent, he pulled on his toes to flex the foot.

All at once, the door behind him was gone and he was falling backward. "Arrrgh!" he cried, both calves knotting with pain as he hit the ground with his head, shoulders, and upper back. His legs still lay across on the seat. Only his flexibility saved him from breaking his back.

"So the prodigal grandson returns. Too bad you're a week too late."

Jeremy recognized that voice. Opening his eyes, he looked up, meeting the icy azure gaze of the one person who would not be happy about his return.

"Hello, Chance."

"About time you came home. She was heartbroken that you never came to see her," Chance said.

He shifted his weight to one leg as he lifted the baseball bat to rest on his shoulder. With his other hand he grabbed Jeremy's upstretched arm. Chance pulled until the other man was out of the car before letting go.

Jeremy sat up and bent forward, grabbing his sneakers

and pulling his toes toward his knees as hard as he could. He groaned as the knotted calf muscles untied themselves, allowing him to think.

Chance stood over him, watching and waiting. He needed some sign that Jeremy shared his pain. Losing Dottie filled Chance's heart with a sharp brittle ache every time he thought of her. It had been her dream to see her grandsons reconcile. She wanted them to move past the anger and hurt that had torn the family to pieces seventeen years before. But her dream had been unfulfilled. And now it was too late.

"I talked to her two weeks ago. Has something happened?"

When the leg cramps eased enough, Jeremy climbed to his feet. He bent in half to stretch the muscles up the back of his legs even further.

"Three days ago she woke up with a strange pain in her foot. But she didn't let that stop her. She collapsed a couple of hours later. We rushed her the hospital, but it was too late. Her lungs filled with fluid and her heart gave out. But as long as she could talk she was asking for you. I called every number in her address book with a New York area code. No one seemed to know how to get in touch with you. It was as if you'd fallen off the face of the earth."

"Yeah, kinda," Jeremy said.

Once his muscles stopped protesting, he straightened and took his first good look at his older brother. He was surprised when he had to lift his chin to look up. When he'd left, Jeremy had been the taller of the two. Now Chance was taller. He'd filled out too, growing into the broad shoulders he'd developed in his early teens. His hair was still black as coal with no signs of silver marring it, and he still wore it long and brushed back from his face. He'd lost the baby fat he'd carried into his twenties. His square chin and movie star dimple were more prominent. There were lines around his eyes and mouth.

"You're looking good, big brother," Jeremy said.

"You look like hell," Chance stated. "Come inside and I'll fix us some breakfast. I don't have any yogurt, kiwi, or fancy dancer food; you'll have to suffer with eggs and toast. The funeral's at eleven." Turning on one heel, Chance headed for the house. He was reeling from the flood of emotions that overflowed his heart. Brotherly concern swelled to fill the place that had been hollow since the night Jeremy left.

Time had been good to Jeremy. He'd remained reed thin with long, supple muscles defining the T-shirt he wore. His hair was shorter now, a deep mahogany brown with golden streaks running through the strands. His tan almost disguised the gray pallor of exhaustion. His golden-flecked hazel eyes hadn't changed, but there was a pain in their depths that Chance could only guess about. Something was eating at his brother's insides.

Chance moved around Dottie's kitchen with the ease of one who'd been there often. He flipped on the coffeemaker he'd given Dottie when her percolator had died. As Jeremy stepped inside, Chance set the fry pan on the stove. He pulled eggs, milk, and bread from the refrigerator. "Set the table," he ordered.

"Sure thing," Jeremy said as he looked around.

The room was still sunshine yellow with bright white trim. The big round table was still covered with a red plaid oilskin tablecloth. Pots of African violets still bloomed above the sink. It was just as he remembered.

The dishes had changed from pressed plastic with wild-flowers to plain white stoneware. They were still in the cupboard next to the sink. The silverware was in the drawer just below. The mismatched coffee mugs were in the same place as well. After setting the table, Jeremy retrieved the ketchup and butter out of the refrigerator.

As soon as the coffee finished brewing, he poured two cups and handed one to his brother. They'd been drinking their coffee black and strong since the month after arriving at Dottie's door. She'd decided that their mother had been coddling them too long. At eleven and thirteen they were old enough to drink coffee. Dottie taught them about coffee, women, gardens, and that dreams gave the dreamer something to aim for. She never told them that dreams might not come true, even with a lifetime of work.

An uneasy tension settled over the room as Jeremy settled into his chair in the corner. Chance set a bowl of scrambled eggs and a plate of toasted bread on the table. He slid into his seat to Jeremy's right and bent his head, his hands folded over his plate.

Jeremy sat silent and still as Chance gave thanks. "Lord, thank you for this food and this day. Teach us to be grateful for all things and to do your work to the best of our ability. Amen."

Jeremy remembered Dottie's prayer as if he too had said it at every meal. The truth was he hadn't prayed since he'd left the last time. Only in extreme conditions did he turn to divine intervention, hoping it would bring a successful end to whatever crisis he faced. Lately he'd been asking for God's help more and more without realizing it.

"You between shows?" Chance asked breaking the silence as he alternated between eggs and toast, chewing rapidly, as if to be done with the meal as soon as possible.

"Not exactly," Jeremy answered, hoping to evade the question for a little longer. "What are you doing these days?"

"Running the Brass Rail and teaching at the Romney

Dance Academy whenever I get a spare hour or two to show them how to hold a proper fifth position."

"So you're still dancing?"

"Not like you, but I'm still able to strut my stuff."

Chance didn't sit back and settle in for a long brother to brother talk. As soon as he finished eating, he carried his plate to the sink and rinsed it. Then he loaded the dishwasher that had been installed where the shelves for Dottie's canned goods had been. Jeremy followed his example.

"The funeral's at eleven. Try not to be late. You can use Dottie's room, but the bed needs clean sheets. I'll be back later." Chance disappeared up the stairs that led to the room they'd shared as children. Before Jeremy could move, Chance reappeared wearing a flannel shirt and a pair of well-worn cowboy boots.

He stalked through the house without another word. The kitchen door closed without a sound behind him, but the screen door slammed as usual. Dottie had always said that she knew who had just run out by listening to that old door. Chance let the door slam behind him, but Jeremy eased it closed as if to sneak away.

Jeremy heard the roar of a motorcycle. The familiar sound sent a chill of loss down Jeremy's spine. He'd sold his to a collector a month after arriving in New York City. The bike brought enough money to pay the rent on his thumbprint-size room and buy food for six months. By the time the money ran out, he'd found a job dancing in an off-off Broadway production. It hadn't been much, but that first job led to another job, then another. Finally he landed a role as a featured performer instead of the fourth guy from the left in the chorus.

So here he was, back in the home of his youth and no one cared. Thankfully, fate had smiled on him enough to deliver him back in time for his grandmother's funeral. What would happen now that his reason for moving back to town was gone?

"Welcome home Jeremy. Make yourself comfortable," he said to himself.

Time to bring in his bags. The boxes could wait until later, but he'd move them to the trunk. No sense tempting anyone to the few boxes of memorabilia he'd kept from his former life.

Dottie was dead. Shock still reverberated through him. He couldn't believe his vibrant, larger-than-life grandmother was gone. He'd have to get to the church early to say his good-byes. This was the day to say goodbye and recognize her long, love-filled life, not to welcome him home.

4

Remi woke, frowning and disoriented, her heart pounding. For a moment she couldn't remember what day it was. Then it came to her: Tuesday. Rolling over, she reached to turn off her alarm clock. Only she'd forgotten to turn it on. And it was almost eight o'clock. She was late for school!

"Oh no," she moaned, throwing off the covers and rolling out of bed in one movement. "Why didn't Mom wake me up?" She pulled off her nightgown and opened the drawer for clean underwear. In less than a minute she was dressed. With her backpack over her shoulder, her comb in one hand and sneakers in the other, she headed for the great room that contained the living room, dining area, and kitchen.

Her mother was sitting at the butcher-block dining table drinking a cup of coffee and flipping through a magazine as if she had all morning to do nothing. She wore her fuzzy yellow robe and looked like she'd been there for awhile.

"Mom, why didn't you wake me up? School started ten minutes ago," Remi cried. She dropped her backpack on the couch and her sneakers on the floor. As she worked the wide-toothed comb through her hair, she shoved her feet into her sneakers.

"Lord, Remi, you scared me," Stacy Applewhite said as she jumped and turned to her daughter. "I didn't wake you because you're not going to school today, remember? Today is Dottie's funeral."

Remi froze. "Oh yeah, I forgot," she whispered, tears filling her eyes at the thought of saying goodbye to her great grandmother.

Stacy stood and went to her. A moment later Remi was wrapped in her mother's arms. She buried her face in the yellow terrycloth of Stacy's robe and began to cry. Remi thought she felt a few tears fall on her hair as well.

Once her tears slowed, Remi pulled away from her mother and wiped her face. "Will it always hurt like this?" she asked. She'd never known anyone who had died. Sure, her friends had lost grandparents, but this was the first time someone in her own family had died.

"Right now the pain is raw and powerful. In time it will hurt less and less. I want you to remember that today is a celebration of her life, not of our loss. Now, let's get you some breakfast. Knowing your dad, he'll be coming by in a little while." Stacy used the sleeve of her robe to dry her own tears. "It's going to be a beautiful, sunny day. Dottie would be pleased."

❧

Chance roared through town on autopilot. Back in high school, whenever he had a problem or an emotion too big to handle, he'd climb on the back of his bike. He always drove like the hounds of hell were chasing him. Sheriff Bolton had called many times, threatening to dismantle the bike if someone didn't teach him to slow down.

That Jeremy had returned home just in time for Dottie's funeral seemed fortuitous. The whole town was no doubt speculating about whether he'd be at the funeral or not. Would his life in New York spare him long enough to bury the woman who'd raised him? Chance hadn't responded to any questions about his brother in seventeen years. Not since the night Jeremy packed up and left town.

Jeremy's Julliard diploma still hung on the living room wall where Dottie had placed it. It didn't take long for people to stop asking, though every time Jeremy's name appeared in *People* magazine or was mentioned on television, Chance heard about it.

Chance never begrudged his little brother his career. He knew Jeremy had worked hard to reach the top of the dance world. He just wished that his brother could have spared more time for his family. There had been times he'd wanted to share news with his brother but couldn't because of the dumb things he'd said. Things he'd regretted as soon as they'd been said out loud. It was too late now. He couldn't retrieve or apologize for things said a decade and a half ago. Pride was sometimes a difficult thing to live with, especially when it got in the way of family.

Revving the engine, Chance flew over the roads. He passed school buses on their morning rounds, pickup trucks, and cars. He tried to out race the anger and the resentment that came from nowhere. His brother had lived his dream while he'd stayed in Romney. His dreams had dried up and blown away like last fall's oak leaves. He'd pushed Jeremy out of the house, daring him to take on New York. He was responsible for making his brother feel that he could not return home before now.

Chance turned on the familiar road, racing around the winding curves up the mountain. He slowed for the dirt road that led to a house he was all too familiar with. Parking in the driveway, he stepped off the bike and ambled toward the front porch. Two women sat on identical wooden rockers, watching his approach.

They could have been bookends they looked so much alike. The blonde hair was natural, hanging at chin length on the older one and below the shoulders on the younger. The brown eyes held the same sad expression, though the younger woman's golden flecks made hers more gold than brown.

They were petite women with dancer's bodies and a love of chocolate. Dressed alike in blue jeans and oversized sweatshirts, they each cupped a mug of what Chance knew to be strong coffee with three sugars and a splash of two percent milk.

Neither moved as he approached. He stopped at the bottom of the three steps that led to the wide porch. With a sigh, he met the older woman's eyes. "He's back," Chance announced.

Stacy's eyes widened. Her cheeks pinked before she swallowed and nodded. "When?"

"Just before dawn. Said he never got our messages."

"But he came back anyway?"

"I think he's in trouble." Chance turned his attention to the younger woman.

At sixteen, she was a carbon copy of her mother, but with her father's passion for dance. Remi was his prize student and his assistant teacher for the youngest students. She knew as much or more than he did about dancing. They should take her to Washington, D.C. for more lessons to further her education, but he was afraid he would lose her like he lost his brother. He couldn't lose Remi. It would tear his heart out.

"You want to ride with me?" he asked, though he already knew her answer.

"Sure. Mom can you bring my dress and my black flats? Oh, and my makeup. Don't forget my makeup." The girl leapt from her rocker and ran inside for her sneakers.

"No makeup!" Chance called after her. "It will only run during the service," he said so only Stacy could hear him.

"Don't worry. I'll forget to bring it." She smiled sadly. "How are you doing?"

Chance turned away looking out over the valley where Romney was nestled and the mountains beyond. He wasn't sure if Stacy was talking about their separation or Dottie's death. In the end it didn't matter.

"It's hard," he said. He swallowed the lump that had grown to basketball size proportions in his throat.

"I know," she said softly. "For me, too."

Before he could ask why they were still apart if it was so hard, Remi emerged. She wore cowboy boots and cradled her electric pink motorcycle helmet under one arm.

"I'm ready."

"Well, let's go. We'll see you at Dottie's later?"

"I'll be there about ten. The minister wants us at the church by ten-thirty," Stacy said.

Chance pulled on his helmet and climbed on board. He steadied the bike while Remi climbed on behind him. Then he started the engine and they were off. The girl wrapped her arms around his middle and held on tight. He drove much slower than when he previously raced out of town, mindful of the precious cargo he carried.

⌇

After settling into Dottie's room and laying out one of the two black suits he'd saved from his former life, Jeremy started snooping. In the seventeen years he'd been gone, little had changed. The furniture and pictures were the same, now forty years out of style. The walls were still bright white, as if Chance had painted in the past year. Even the room he and Chance had shared under the eaves hadn't changed. Chance hadn't redecorated as he outgrew the posters of bikini-clad girls they'd plastered on the walls.

That's when Jeremy saw the suitcase. It took up half of the six-foot long table the boys had shared as a desk. Shifting the suitcase to one side, he wasn't surprised to find the white first aid tape that marked the center of the table. Why would Chance be living out of a suitcase?

Chance had said he owned businesses in town. He must not have moved too far away.

Turning to scan the rest of the room, the picture frame over Chance's bed caught his eye. It was almost as big as the sexy starlet poster that used to hang there. An inch of brighter white wall highlighted the gold frame, drawing the eye to its contents.

A collage of pictures surrounded a central eight by ten. In it Chance looked uncomfortable but happy in a navy blue suit with his arm around his bride who wore an ivory colored floor length dress with a foot wide ruffle at the hem and lace at the collar and sleeves. Her blonde hair was fluffed and teased and sprayed away from her pale face, revealing elfin features and a nervous smile. Jeremy sucked in his breath.

Stacy Smith. Chance had married *his* girlfriend. At least she had been his girlfriend before he'd disappeared from Romney in the middle of the night. The picture was dated two months after his departure. What was going on?

Jeremy scanned the rest of the pictures that tracked the history of his brother's life: the grand opening of the Brass Rail Restaurant and Lounge, the opening of the dance school, and Stacy's pregnancy. Then there were baby pictures and family pictures as the baby grew from a sandy-haired toddler into a young woman. In the latest one, she was flying through the air like a gazelle. The joy of dance glowed on her sweat-dampened face. She wore practice clothes, not the frilly, lacy costume of a stage performance. The girl had inherited her uncle's love of dancing.

"Her name is Remi." The feminine voice caught him off guard as his fingers traced the girl's flying form, marveling at the height of the jump.

Jeremy straightened and turned to face the first love of his life. "Hello, Stacy."

She hadn't changed in the time he'd been gone. She was still a pixie of a woman with her blonde hair cut into a chin length style with bangs that almost covered her eyes. It was caught behind the tiniest, most delicate ears that had ever been attached to a woman's head. She wore gold studs instead of the large hoops she'd favored years ago.

She wasn't surprised to find him here. Had Chance called her, warned her that Jackass Jeremy was back in town?

"Hello, Jeremy. You're looking well," she said.

She crossed the room and hung two hangers over the closet door. The first held a blue suit. If Jeremy had to guess, it was the same suit Chance had worn in the wedding photograph seventeen years before. The second held a navy blue dress. Since Stacy was already wearing a black suit with jewel neck white blouse beneath, Jeremy assumed that Remi would be wearing this dress.

"I'd suggest you go on downstairs if you don't want Chance to throw you out that window," Stacy said.

Jeremy nodded. He preceded the woman out of the room that brought back so many memories. He had a thousand questions he wanted to ask, but wasn't sure if Stacy was the one to answer them.

They had just entered the living room when he heard the kitchen door open.

⌘

Chance didn't drive straight back to town. Instead, he drove the back roads. Early morning sun flashed through the trees where it could. The air took on a nip when driving forty-five miles per hour. He took comfort in Remi clinging to his back. This was one of the things he'd missed most about not living at home; riding with his girl, her arms wrapped around his middle and cheek resting between his shoulder blades. They never talked, just enjoyed the time together as they rode for miles over the back roads of West Virginia. Riding through the county with Stacy or Remi was when Chance was most at peace.

The digital clock he'd added to the bike's control panel blinked 8:45 at him. It was time to return to town. Time to face the sorrows and pain and responsibilities of the day. Revving the engine, he flew through town, slowing to turn into Dottie's driveway.

"Cool car!" Remi gushed, pulling off her helmet as she danced around the Mercedes. "Whose is it?"

"Your Uncle Jeremy's. He pulled in early this morning. I want you to behave and not ambush him with a thousand and one questions," Chance said. He took the girl's helmet and secured it to the back of the motorcycle.

"Would I do that?" Remi tossed over her shoulder as she leapt onto the porch.

"Honey, I'm never sure what you might do," Chance said. He ruffled her hair and was surprised when she squealed "Dad!" and began to brush her hair back into place.

Chance felt a twinge of sorrow at losing his dancing tomboy. Soon boys would start lining up at the front door, begging for her attention. Maybe having Jeremy back in town wouldn't be so bad after all. He could help chaperone dates and threaten prospective suitors. That is, if he stayed around.

Entering the kitchen behind Remi, Chance was surprised to see the dishes put away and the kitchen put back to rights. So Jeremy wasn't the slob he'd been as a teenager. What other surprises would the next few days hold? Would he find out that his brother wasn't the monster of Chance's memories?

5

*R*emi froze in the middle of the kitchen. She was about to meet the most famous person ever to live in Romney. Knowing he was her uncle only added to her awe. Her stomach clenched, her heart pounded, and she hoped she wouldn't embarrass herself by asking all the questions she had about dancing, New York, and how to start her career.

All at once she wasn't so sure she wanted to meet her uncle. But it was too late. Her father had taken her hand and was leading her into the living room.

Jeremy met Chance's eyes when he entered the living room. There was a warning in them. Was he warning him away from Stacy? Or from the girl? Or was there another reason his brother's intense eyes were hard, cold chips of blue ice?

When Jeremy cocked his head in silent query, Chance broke eye contact and turned to the woman beside him. Jeremy watched as those same eyes warmed to pieces of warm summer sky as he gazed at Stacy. "Does this mean we're late?"

"Not yet. I just got here." Stacy shifted, uncomfortable with the tension in the room. "You feel better?"

"Yeah, I guess." Shifting, Chance pulled the girl up to stand beside him. "Remi, this is your uncle, Jeremy Applewhite. Jeremy, this is our daughter, Remi."

"Hello," Remi said in a tone just above a whisper. Jeremy had to strain to hear her.

"Hi," Jeremy replied, his lips curving. Like all young dancers he'd met in the last years, this young lady had a thousand questions to ask about dancing and New York and the world. He could see them in her eyes.

Remi glanced at her mother, then her father, then lowered her eyes to the floor. "I'd better get changed." With that she slipped past her father and up the stairs.

"She's beautiful," Jeremy commented to the room at large. "She moves like a dancer."

"Yeah, she is. I don't want you filling her head with crazy fantasies. She's a small town girl and I don't want her crushed."

Jeremy's glance at his brother could have cut glass. He wanted to punch him right in the middle of his chest. Or maybe a good shot to the head would clear his thinking.

"The world outside Romney isn't something to be feared, Chance. Someday you'll have to let her discover life for herself."

Chance sucked in a breath and held it for a long time. He released it again. "I've got to get a shower," he said. He stalked to the bathroom, closing the door with enough force for the air to shiver around Jeremy and Stacy.

"Would you like some coffee?" Stacy asked. She didn't wait for his answer before rushing into the kitchen to put on a fresh pot.

"Well, that was buckets of fun," Jeremy muttered. He walked around the room. Nothing had changed except the pictures sitting on the top of the upright piano. His high school graduation picture had been replaced by one of his latest publicity stills. Chance's picture was a family portrait with Stacy and Remi.

Taking a deep breath, Jeremy rubbed his eyes with the heels of his hands. He ran his fingers through his hair and bent backward in a stretch. There were secrets here, secrets and pain and broken dreams that had piled up, forming a wall that now separated him from the only family he had left. He had to find a way over, around, or through that wall. If he couldn't, he might as well climb back into his car and drive away.

In Dottie's room, Jeremy changed from sweats into the black suit. He debated on a hat and sunglasses but decided against them. Dottie would have wanted to see him, not a shield. Slipping on his most comfortable black sneakers, he picked up his keys and wallet.

The shower was still running when he'd finished dressing. He sat down on the side of Dottie's bed and let sorrow wash over him.

He'd made so many mistakes. He should have come back sooner. He should have been here for her. He should have mended fences with Chance years ago. Somehow, he had to get Chance to talk to him. Maybe together they could figure out how to be a family again.

His eyes filled with tears that he tried to blink away. One escaped, sliding slowly down his face. He didn't bother to brush it away. Before the day was over, he would shed more. He might as well relieve the pressure behind his eyes now, so he wouldn't become a blubbering idiot in front of the entire town.

"Uncle Jeremy? Mom wants to know how you take your coffee," Remi said from the doorway.

"Black's fine," Jeremy replied, brushing at his cheek.

"You okay?" she asked. She stopped beside the bed where Jeremy sat, elbows on widespread knees, hands clasped.

Jeremy lifted his head and stared. The girl was a near perfect image of her mother. "No, Remi, I'm not. I'm just not sure what to do to make things right." Tears glittered, then ran down his cheeks. His emotions bubbled over, an active volcano.

Remi blinked fast, trying to keep her own tears from overflowing. Sitting down next to him, she wrapped one arm around his back. "Dottie is in Heaven now. She's not in pain. She's not feeling old and useless. She's with her husband and her friends and her children. But she's also with us in our memories," Remi said. She leaned her temple against his shoulder. "It's okay to cry. It helps clean out the tear ducts and wash the eyes."

Jeremy shifted so he could return her embrace. "How did you get so wise?"

"The Learning Channel on cable," Remi said. Her tone was so serious that Jeremy had to laugh.

"Romney's got cable? Wow, they're really moving into the twenty-first century, aren't they?"

"We even have computers at the high school. I can't wait until next semester when I get to take another computer class and driver's ed. I'm just not sure which path to follow. Academic or career training."

The shower cut off just beyond the bedroom wall. Jeremy stood, and pulled Remi to her feet. He needed coffee. "What do you want to be when you grow up?"

"Employed," Remi answered with a straight face. When her uncle looked at her with surprise, she began to giggle. "Mom told me to use that as my stock answer until I figure out what I want to be. That way I'll appear wise beyond my years."

"Your mom used to use that on people when she was your

age," Jeremy said as they entered the kitchen.

"I used what when I was her age?" Stacy asked. She turned from the refrigerator where she was pulling plastic containers out and dumping the leftovers in the garbage.

"You wanted to be employed when you grew up," Jeremy said. He slid into his chair and smiled a thank you when Remi slid a mug of hot, black coffee in front of him.

"Ah, yes." She settled into the chair across the table with her own mug. "So Jeremy, what do you want to be when you grow up?"

"I've had my dream. Now I have to come up with a job for the rest of my life," Jeremy answered before taking a sip of coffee. He swallowed, sighed, and sipped again. Stacy still made the best coffee he'd ever tasted.

Jeremy studied the two women at the table. Remi had inherited Stacy's hair and chin and mouth. He didn't see anything of Chance. Her eyes weren't the intense azure, but were green and gold and brown swirled together.

Just then Chance stepped into the room. "Any coffee left?"

Stacy was pouring his cup before he'd finished his question. She placed it before him as he slid into his seat, then stood behind him. Jeremy saw longing in her eyes.

He watched the interaction without comment. There was more going on here than anyone would admit to.

Sipping his coffee, Jeremy brooded. Looking at Stacy, his heart turned over in his chest. It was the same as when he was in tenth grade. He'd confessed his feelings to her after the Sadie Hawkins dance in February. She hadn't answered him, just gotten a strange look on her face and brushed a kiss across his cheek.

He'd told her often of his love. She'd never returned the sentiment. Had she been in love with Chance even then? Is that why they'd married so soon after he'd left town? More questions he was afraid to ask. Finding out that the truth would be painful, even after seventeen years.

Jeremy excused himself from the table and returned to Dottie's bedroom. Opening the top drawer of her dresser, he pulled out a handkerchief. She'd never been without one of these fine Irish linen with delicate edgings in different colors. He bypassed the pinks and purples, instead pulling out two with blue crocheted lace around the edges. He put one in each jacket pocket. Picking up two with yellow lace, he returned to the kitchen. It was time to go.

"Want to ride with me?" he asked Remi.

"Sure!" Remi said. She carried her glass to the sink and rinsed it.

"We'll meet you at the church. Or would you like to come with us?" Jeremy asked Stacy.

"No, we'll walk over from here. But we'll ride with you to the cemetery, if that's okay," she answered.

"Sure." With a sad smile, Jeremy turned and followed his niece out of the kitchen.

ॐ

Chance waited until he heard the purr of the sleek Mercedes fade away before he spoke. "So what do we have to talk about that can't wait until after Jeremy leaves town?"

"What makes you think he'll be leaving?"

"Why would he stay? Dottie's gone. His life is in New York or London or wherever his latest show is playing. He'll die of boredom if he stays here long," Chance said. His stomach knotted at the thought of Jeremy staying longer than a week. How could he compete with his famous brother? Especially for Remi's affection. At sixteen, the girl loved him one day and hated him the next.

"So do we tell him?" Stacy asked. It was the one question neither wanted to think about.

"I don't want him disrupting Remi's life any more than necessary. As it is, I bet he's filling her head with the excitement of life on the Broadway stage. Come on, I don't want to leave them alone any longer I have to," Chance said. He pushed out of his chair. He carried their coffee mugs to the sink while Stacy retrieved her purse.

Chance took her hand as they crossed the porch and stepped down into the yard. "God, I miss Dottie," he whispered as they stepped onto the path and turned toward town.

6

*J*eremy drove through town slowly. He noted the changes he'd missed during the middle of the night. He waited for Remi to bombard him with questions. But she didn't speak. She sat in her seat, staring at him, an expression of awe in her gold-flecked eyes.

Glancing in the rearview mirror, he realized where he'd seen those eyes before. Every time he looked in a mirror they looked back at him. His niece had his eyes.

"Am I turning purple or growing a second head?" he asked. He turned the corner in front of the First Methodist Church of Romney. He'd have to go around the block and come back to fall in line behind the hearse.

"Nothing like that. I just can't believe you're here. I mean, you've been around the world and danced for the President and Oprah and everything," she gushed.

"They're people, just like you and me."

"You're not like anyone else in Romney. You're famous!" Remi argued.

Jeremy wanted to disagree but didn't know how. How could he voice the fear that his life, like his career, was at an end? He could hardly admit the truth to himself. How was he to explain it to this child whose life stretched out in front of her?

"What are you planning to do once you graduate from

high school?" he asked. "I saw a picture at Dottie's of you dancing. Are you interested in dancing as a career?"

"I'd love it, but Dad says I couldn't survive in the big city. I'm small town born and raised. I'm probably not good enough anyway," she said. She sounded resigned to a life without her dream

"I'd like to see you dance," Jeremy said.

"I'm at the studio every afternoon, either practicing or teaching the little ones." Golden brown eyes went from dull to brilliant in two heartbeats.

"We'll have to talk to your teacher, but I don't see why I couldn't help out," Jeremy said.

He left plenty of room behind the silvery gray hearse. The sadness of the day sunk in as he stared at the vehicle in front of them.

"Dottie's already inside the church, isn't she?" Remi asked.

"Yes, I'm sure she is," Jeremy said. He pulled one of the linen handkerchiefs trimmed in yellow from his pocket. "I think she'd like you to use this today."

"She always carried one of these tucked in her pocket," Remi said. Holding it to her nose, she took a deep breath. "It still smells like her."

"Here's one for your mom," Jeremy said. "Can you stay out here for a few minutes? I need to go inside to say my goodbyes alone."

"I'm sixteen, not six, Uncle Jeremy. I'll be fine. Mom and Dad will be here soon" Remi said. She unbuckled her seatbelt and shifted in her seat. "I'll wait here."

"Thanks, kiddo." Jeremy patted her shoulder, the motion feeling awkward.

His sneakers made no sound as he crossed the sidewalk

and four steps to the church's porch. Stepping inside, he pulled off his sunglasses and blinked in the dim light.

The double doors to the sanctuary stood open, inviting visitors inside. A young man stood in the doorway. He wore a black suit, silver-gray shirt, and burgundy tie. Fashionable yet a couple of years out of date, he exuded an aura of authority. He also looked too young to be the minister or the funeral home director. When Jeremy paused several feet from the doorway, he stepped forward.

"May I help you?" he asked in a hushed tone.

"I'd like a few minutes alone with my grandmother," Jeremy said. He looked into the sanctuary, his gaze locked on the glossy wooden casket.

"You're grandmother? But I thought..." the man paused. "Of course, you're Jeremy. Welcome home. I'm glad you could make it." Extending a hand, his polite smile notched up several degrees. "I'm Matthew Hawk. No one's here yet, so you have some time."

"Thanks," Jeremy murmured. He moved past the other man into the church's sanctuary.

The center aisle was wide, and the sun shining through the stained glass windows created colorful islands on the carpet. Half the casket was open to prove that Dottie was the occupant. His steps slowed as his grandmother's profile came into view. Like her house and this town, she hadn't changed that much.

Her glasses were still gold-rimmed frames. Her hair was silvery-white, the last strands of black having lost the fight against advancing age. The pin curls she'd styled on soft pink foam rollers hadn't changed. Her skin was smoother than he remembered.

He remembered the rose-colored dress. She'd worn that

to church every other Sunday. On alternating weeks, she wore a deep turquoise one of the same style. She'd made the dresses. She'd made all the dresses hanging in her closet.

Self-sufficient should have been Dottie Applewhite's middle name. She'd had a garden, canned her own food, made her own clothes, and even shoveled her own coal. If necessary, she could have rebuilt her own house from the ground up had a storm carried it away.

She wore only three pieces of jewelry: her gold wedding band, the ruby ring her husband had given her on their fortieth wedding anniversary, and the gold circle pin Jeremy had given her his last Christmas at home.

"Oh, Dottie, I wish... I wish... Why couldn't I have come home a week earlier? I wish you could have seen me dance," he said. He reached out to touch her. He paused, his fingers just an inch from the back of her hand. He still couldn't believe she'd passed away.

"She did see you," Chance said a moment before a hand settled on his left shoulder. "Last Christmas at the Kennedy Center."

Jeremy looked over his shoulder at his brother. "Why didn't she come backstage?"

Chance blinked back his tears. "She had waited so long for you to come home or invite her to New York. She didn't want to be a bother. After the performance, we came straight home. She talked about that evening for months. She was so proud of you. Whenever you danced on television, we taped the shows. She'd watch them for hours."

"I wish I'd known. I screwed up, big time." Jeremy said. He sniffled and wiped at the tears that began to flow. "How do I make this up?"

"You can't. Her only regret was that you hadn't returned

home. Stacy and Remi are certain she's here in spirit and knows that you're here. And knowing that, she's content."

Dottie couldn't forgive him, but Jeremy had to find a way to crawl back into Chance's good graces. They were all each other had. They were the last of the Applewhites. Only that wasn't true any longer. Chance had Stacy and Remi.

Taking a shuddering breath, Jeremy turned and hugged Chance. "How are we ever going to get along without her?"

Chance didn't return the embrace immediately, but finally his arms came up to wrap around his brother. "I don't know. One way or another we have to try," Chance said. A moment later they separated. It wouldn't do for the minister and half the town to find the Applewhite brothers holding each other up as they sobbed.

"What are your plans?" Chance asked, wanting to change the subject to anything that didn't involve Dottie or death. He turned away so Jeremy wouldn't see his pain, his longing to have his brother close again.

"My plans? I don't think I have any. Not until this day is over. Then I'll think about the future." Jeremy said. He wiped his eyes, then blew his nose on a tissue he pulled from his pocket. He'd save Dottie's handkerchiefs for later.

Chance nodded, but didn't respond. He didn't know how.

⁊

Remi sat between her parents in the front row of the church during the service that was meant to celebrate her great-grandmother's life. She'd been to only one funeral before, that of a friend of her mother when she was about ten. But that woman did not have nearly as many people as Dottie's did. Just before the service, she'd turned around and saw that every pew in the church was filled, and there were people lined up along the walls. Turning back around, she vowed not to cry.

That promise lasted only until the organist began to play the first hymn. The familiar notes of "Amazing Grace" filled the church, and tears rolled down Remi's face. She couldn't stop them, so she pulled out the handful of tissues her mother had given her. She didn't want to use Dottie's linen handkerchief. She would keep that as a reminder of the woman who had taught her to dream big, then work on ways to make her dreams come true.

As friends stood and spoke lovingly about the woman everyone in town knew and loved, Remi looked around. Both her mother and father were crying. She heard sniffling and crying and blowing noses coming from all corners of the room. Even the minister looked misty-eyed as he said the final prayer and dismissed the crowd to go to the graveside, then return to the church for lunch that had been prepared by the women of the church.

⌒

By the time Jeremy pulled the car into the driveway at Dottie's house, he was exhausted. He hadn't felt so limp since the night he'd performed in a three-hour Broadway musical with a one-hundred-one degree temperature. This was worse because his emotions were shredded as well. He'd shaken hands with just about every woman and most of the men in town. He'd heard tales from his grandmother's childhood up through what she'd baked for the church bazaar the week before.

Turning off the car engine, he dropped his head back against the headrest. He took a deep breath, hoping to find the energy to climb from the car and walk into the house.

"Remi, help me carry this food into the house," Stacy said. She sounded tired.

"I'll help, but then I have to go by the restaurant," Chance said. He opened his door and climbed out, following the women to the trunk. The leftovers from the post-funeral luncheon were packed in plastic containers in the trunk.

Jeremy popped the button to release the trunk, then climbed out. "There's enough food here to feed an army for a month," he observed.

"Yeah, but it's *so* good," Remi replied, picking up the box with three pies in it. She glanced down, longing for a fork.

"They're the last thing you should eat as a dancer. Big hips are not in this year," Jeremy teased.

Once the food was put away, Chance headed for the back door. "I've got to go to work. I'll be back about midnight."

"I've got to get to the studio. The kids will understand why Chance isn't there, but not why the studio isn't open," Stacy said, reaching for her purse.

"Can I come?" Jeremy asked. He had no plans, no work, no worries, no life. Dancing would help pass the time and would help him clear his mind.

"Sure, but it won't be what you're used to," Stacy said.

"Give me two minutes to change," Jeremy said. He slipped from the room, looking forward to an afternoon with a group of young, passionate dancers.

Was his ego really in such a state that he needed to show off for a group of babies? He pushed the question away, not wanting to know the truth.

7

The Applewhite Dance Studio was in one of the few houses that qualified for mansion status in Romney. It was on Main Street, two blocks east of the courthouse. The Governor's mansion. Jeremy thought when he drove up the driveway past the discreet sign in the front yard. How could Chance afford this place? The house was Romney's other claim to fame. In 1890, the governor wanted a house that would outshine the rest of the state. Floor to ceiling windows on the first floor, a grand ballroom on the third, and plenty of room for his many children did just that.

Pulling into the parking space next to Stacy, he turned off the engine and grabbed his bag. Inside were spare clothes, shoes, a couple of bottles of water, and snacks. Climbing out of the car, he swung the black bag over one shoulder.

Remi grabbed his hand and pulled him along behind her. "Come on, Uncle Jeremy!" she urged. "I can't wait to see you dance."

Her excitement was contagious. "We'll see about me dancing after classes are over. Now, where is the studio?"

"Upstairs," Remi said. She led the way through the front door, turning right and heading up a side set of stairs. Jeremy had to hurry to follow her to the third floor.

Stacy followed at a more leisurely pace, not sure she could get through the afternoon. She was sure she would confess her crimes to Jeremy. She'd always been able to talk to the amber-eyed man. They never fought, except for that last night, the night he'd left town.

"Don't think about it," she said to herself. "There's nothing you can do about it now, so don't think about it."

As they reached the third floor, a swarm of three-foot tall pink and black clad pixies surrounded them. "Miz Applewhite, you're here!" Jenny Mulroy grabbed her hand. "Can we warm up now?"

"Go on inside and find your spots while Remi and I change. We'll start in a few minutes," Stacy said.

"Come on, girls, show me around," Jeremy said.

"Who are you?" Jenny asked, wary of the tall man. Just because he was good-looking didn't mean they should go with him. He was a stranger and they'd all been warned about strangers.

"This is my Uncle Jeremy. Remember we watched the video about him last month? If you're good, maybe he'll teach us something special to dance for the recital," Remi said.

They crowded around him. Each girl wanted to touch the famous Jeremy Applewhite. After all, he'd been on television. In seconds, the fear and distrust turned to acceptance. The girls led him into their classroom, bombarding him with questions and information about themselves.

🖎

Remi loved dancing. She loved the moves, the music, and the freedom of expression when she was allowed to make up her own dances. She also loved teaching the youngest classes. Her mom did the real teaching, but Remi worked with a few of the girls as well. Today, while Stacy worked on the gliding side-step across the room with the main class, Remi's attention was divided between Jeremy and the two little girls who had become her very own dance class.

Tina and Rachel were slower than the other girls and less coordinated but loved to dance just as much. Remi was trying to teach them the same gliding side-step, but the girls were having a hard time following her. They kept stumbling or stepping on their own feet.

"Remi, could I made a suggestion?" Jeremy had been watching and could feel the growing frustration that she had to keep under control.

"Sure," she said, hoping he would not embarrass her for being a bad teacher.

Jeremy joined them and looked down at Tina. "Would you like to dance with me?" he asked.

"Okay," Tina said. She was the more daring of the two, willing to try anything and sometimes too bold for her own good.

"Hold my hands," Jeremy bent over and held his hands out to the tiny redhead. She took hold, though her hands could only span three of his fingers.

Remi held her hands out to Rachel and they followed Jeremy and Tina, who side-stepped across the room at a slow pace. At this point they weren't gliding, just stepping. "Step, together. Step, together," she said, keeping pace with their slow steps. The trip back across the room was done just as slowly. Their next pass was faster, and by the end of class, the girls were gliding on their own almost as fast as the rest of the students.

"Thanks," she told her uncle as the end-of-class chaos erupted. She had to smile when Tina was able to show her mother what she'd learned in class.

"You're welcome," Jeremy said. "Reminds me of a class I helped out with when I was getting started in New York a long, long time ago."

⤳

By the time Stacy turned off the lights, Jeremy had learned a new respect for dance teachers. He normally danced four hours a day. Today he'd taught as well as given demonstrations of proper stance or style for four classes of increasingly taller dancers. He was exhausted.

When the last of the dancers, a group of five star-struck young women, filed out, Jeremy collapsed in the middle of the floor. All he wanted was a hot shower and his bed. He was completely drained.

"You still alive?" Stacy crossed the room and stopped beside him. She moved with the same dancer's grace she'd always had. Jeremy opened his eyes and studied her for a long moment.

"Why didn't you come with me?" he asked softly.

Stacy swallowed the lump in her throat. Then she blinked twice at the bewildered innocence of his tone. He sounded lost and confused, like he didn't understand why she hadn't thrown some clothes in a bag, climbed on the back of his motorcycle, and flown away in the middle of the night.

"I was two months away from graduating from high school. Did you really think I'd pick up and run away because you demanded it?"

She folded in upon herself, sinking to the floor. She pulled her knees to her chest and wrapped her arms around them, careful to keep two feet of highly polished floor between her toes and Jeremy's hip. Thankfully, he didn't see her expression. He remained flat on his back on the floor. His eyes were closed and his arms stretched out to the sides.

He remained silent for so long that she thought he'd fallen asleep. She wouldn't have blamed him. It had been a long day.

He was probably still reeling from Dottie's death.

"So what happened? You married Chance two days after graduating from high school. Why didn't you come to New York?" His soft-spoken questions sent arrows straight through her heart.

Dropping her head to her knees, she couldn't answer. Instead, she pushed to her feet. Without another sound, she slipped from the room. She wiped away the tears that overflowed without warning.

It took two minutes to change into her street clothes and pack her sweaty dance outfit. She hoped Jeremy would leave before she exited the dressing room. With flight foremost in her mind, she peeked out of the dressing room and found the hallway to the staircase empty. Good, he was already gone. She slipped out and down the stairs.

$$\sim$$

After working the late shift at the Brass Rail, Chance drove through town to the dance studio. He didn't have time for dancing these days, but some nights it felt good to put his body through its paces. Most people would think he was crazy for wanting to exert himself after a busy night, but it was just what Chance needed. Dancing would untie the knots that had been growing across his shoulders and up his neck ever since Dottie's death.

Turning into the driveway, Chance was surprised to find the lights on in the third floor windows of the Governor's mansion. Was Stacy still working? Or had Remi stayed late to practice a new routine?

Pulling into his space, he was surprised to see Jeremy's car. Had he come to watch the classes? Or just to be near Stacy? Was he the one dancing in the wee hours of the morning?

Using his key, Chance let himself in the back door, careful to lock it behind him. The ladies of the Hampshire Historical Society and Romney Community Arts Council fussed at him every time he left the door unlocked.

He paused at the top of the stairs. There was no music coming from the studio. Stopping at the doorway, he was surprised to find his brother laid out flat in the middle of the floor.

Jeremy wore close fitting black sweats and a red shirt that highlighted the tanned muscles of his arms. He was barefoot, which was surprising. With the classes of younger dancers, Chance was tempted to wear steel-toed boots. But then he remembered dancing barefoot across the wooden floor of the Cumberland Dance Studio, how he felt free when callused feet met polished wood.

But that was years ago. Nowadays, Chance wore extra-stiff arch supports in his shoes, even when dancing.

Ducking into the dressing room, Chance changed into his dance clothes. "Hey, sleepyhead," he said, nudging Jeremy's thigh with the toe of his dance shoe.

The body on the floor moaned, then grew still again.

"Jeremy, wake up. I want to dance and you're a big ugly lump on the floor."

"What? Who? Why?" Jeremy said. He jerked upright, his forehead smashing into Chance's chin. "Ouch! What are you doing?"

"Trying to wake you up to dance with me." Chance rubbed at his chin. He began stretching, flexing the muscles of his legs.

"What time is it?" Jeremy asked. He shifted to face his brother, mirroring his movements.

"Who cares? You're awake, I'm awake, and now we can dance."

Jeremy was exhausted and fuzzy-brained from lack of sleep and the stress of the day. But looking at his brother in his red sweats and white T-shirt, he knew he was being challenged. Chance had an unholy gleam in his eyes that said he was looking for blood.

They shifted back and forth, stretching and warming each set of muscles and tendons, one after the other. They moved through the routine of warming up as if time had slipped and they were teenagers again.

Finally Chance felt limber. He stood and crossed to the sound system. His favorite CD was still in the CD player. "Follow the leader?"

Jeremy nodded, hoping he could keep up. His knees were screaming. His sleep-deprived brain was wrapped in cotton, and after one look at his brother's expression, he wondered if he would survive.

"You leading or following?" He finally asked, though he knew Chance would lead. At least in the beginning. Eventually Jeremy would have his opportunity to choreograph their moves.

As one, they turned to the mirror. Chance took two steps forward while Jeremy stepped back. Mentally they divided the floor down the middle and each would dance on his half. That was one of the unspoken rules held over from childhood. It also kept them from slamming into or tripping each other.

Chance listened to the music then began to move, his feet flying in combinations of steps based on the same gliding motion that Jeremy had taught Tina just hours before. They danced in silence, each concentrating on the steps and the music. Jeremy tried not to think about all that had happened in the last twenty-four hours. He'd danced profession-

ally long enough that he could follow anyone's lead without
thinking about what he was doing. He had turned into a dancing robotic machine that anyone could program, as long as
music played in the background.

He mimicked Chance's increasingly complex movements
so closely that he looked like his brother's shadow. His body
busy keeping pace and changing easily from ballet music to
jazz songs to fast tapping tunes to modern rock-and-roll—
his mind drifted back seventeen years.

8

He'd come home during spring break for Dottie's birthday. He took the train from New York to Washington, D.C. and then the bus to Romney. After four days of vacation, he was looking forward to returning to New York. He needed to be where a night owl could find a good pizza after midnight and where classes, rehearsals, and auditions dominated his life.

Two days after Dottie's birthday party, Stacy played hooky and spent the day with him. His time in Romney was almost over, and he didn't want to say goodbye. Going back after Christmas break, he'd been depressed for days. He couldn't imagine how hard it would be to survive until Stacy graduated and moved to New York.

March was still a winter month in West Virginia. But Mother Nature smiled, giving them blue skies and spring-like temperatures. They'd picked up burgers and fries from the only fast food joint in twenty miles, then went to Moyer's Apple Orchard just east of town and had a picnic under the trees. Their heated petting sessions had taken them to the edge of loving before, but never over.

"Do it, Jeremy. Love me," she'd whispered in his ear.

Jeremy wanted to pause, to back up and take a breath, but he couldn't. His brain shut down. His body took over.

Later, he asked, "Why? I thought you were saving yourself." His voice was low as he shifted until they were again two entities. Wrapping his arms around her, one high on her shoulders, the other across her hips, he rolled so he lay cushioning her from the hard ground.

Stacy never raised her head to look at him. All he could see was her shoulder length, honey blonde hair. She remained silent for a long time. "Because I love you, and I'm your woman, and I couldn't wait any longer," she said.

She lifted her head and looked at him. Her eyes were bright with tears, her expression joy filled. He'd expected her to regret her decision, to call back the last hour.

"Come with me," he said. He wanted nothing more than to climb on his motorcycle with her and head to New York City.

"Go with you?" she asked.

"Yeah, come back with me."

"What about school? I've only got a couple of months left."

"I can't leave you behind again. Come with me. You can finish school there."

Stacy rolled off of him and sat up. Jeremy watched as she dressed, her bra twisted, her T-shirt inside out. "I can't leave now. I'll be valedictorian of the class if I can keep my grades up. I'm giving a speech at graduation. Mama and Daddy would die if I left now. I'll be the first member of the family to actually finish high school."

"It's not important. What's important is us being together."

"Jeremy Applewhite, my life is just as important as yours. I can't believe you want me to give up what I've been working toward for thirteen years of my life."

Jeremy sat up and eased her down into his lap. He pulled her shirt off of her, undid her bra, straightened out the twists, and dressed her again. When she was dressed, he pulled on his own clothes. They climbed onto the bike without another word, and he drove her home. It was time to return to real life.

"I love you," he called after her. She raced across the front yard of her parents' home and didn't hear him. Instead, she slammed into the house without a backward glance.

Jeremy roared off. He headed out of town, racing the wind through the mountains. The woman he'd just spent the afternoon loving didn't love him enough to come with him.

By the time he finally arrived home, the dinner hour had passed and the sun had long since set. Jeremy was shivering from the rapidly cooling temperatures. He predicted winter would be making a return visit.

Chance was waiting for him on the porch wearing his winter coat. "What the hell did you do to Stacy?" he asked. He pushed out of the swing and stood with his arms crossed over his chest. This was where Dottie snapped beans and shelled peas. It was where the boys came to be alone. This back porch was where Jeremy spent nearly a third of his life.

"What's it to you?" Jeremy said, giving in to the black mood he'd fallen into.

"Her mother called and said you dropped her off four hours ago, and she's been crying ever since. Mrs. Smith is afraid their house is going to flood. You look like you lost your last friend. What the hell did you do to Stacy?"

"None of your damn business," Jeremy growled.

He launched himself at his brother. Chance took his weight, but they crashed into the flowerbed that skirted the porch. They rolled out onto the grass, grunted, and *oomphed* when an occasional punch connected. Chance accepted Jeremy's abuse but got in a few licks of his own. All the while he asked repeatedly why Stacy was drowning her mother in tears.

By the time his emotions were played out, Jeremy felt like a punching bag. He was also ashamed. Not only had he accepted Stacy's virginity, now he'd beaten on his brother instead of sharing his heartbreak. With a sigh, he climbed to his feet and walked away. His body was sore and his heart ached. It was time to leave.

After a hot shower that only heightened his awareness of his bruises, Jeremy retreated to his room. He threw everything he thought he might need into his duffle bag. He tried to write a note to Dottie but couldn't find the words to explain. After pulling on the wool sweater Dottie had knitted him for Christmas, he grabbed his jacket and duffle bag and headed out. He paused in the living room. Chance was in the shower, and Dottie had gone to bed an hour before.

With a deep breath, Jeremy pulled on his jacket and walked out the door, begging forgiveness from both Stacy and Chance.

♪

Jeremy returned to the present with a painful jolt, coming down after a high grand jeté his left knee refused to hold his weight. He stumbled, off balance. He recovered before falling face first to the floor. Pain radiated from knee to hip to lower back. He'd overdone it. It was time to quit for the day.

When Jeremy stumbled and fell, Chance stopped dancing as well. "You okay?" he asked.

He crossed to where his brother stood on his right leg, his left one extended out in front of him. He wore an unreadable blank expression. His breathing was harsh from the exertion, but his cheeks were almost gray beneath his tan.

"Just growing old," Jeremy replied gloomily.

Not knowing what to expect, Jeremy held onto the wooden barre and slowly shifted his weight to his left leg. But the knee refused to cooperate. Using the barre for support, he lowered himself to the floor.

Pulling on the Velcro that held his pants together, he peeled the worn material away from his lower leg. His knee looked like black, purple, blue, and red crayons that had melted together inside a plastic bag. The retirement he'd been trying not to think about seemed to be now a rather grim probability.

His doctors had been warning him for two years to quit the rigorous performing and rehearsal schedule he'd maintained. But he'd ignored their warnings. He was still young by most people's standards, but for a dancer he was an old, old man.

Examining his knee without actually touching it, Jeremy realized the truth. His career was over and the rest of his life was about to begin, whether he was ready or not.

Chance bent over his brother and sucked in a sharp breath. "Holy shit, Jeremy. That knee looks like hell. Should I call Doc Spencer?"

"No, no doctor. Just help me to my car. I'll ice it down and it'll be good as new by morning," Jeremy said. The lie, issued through clenched teeth, didn't fool either brother, but self-delusion was all he had left.

"Okay, it's way past time to close up anyway." Chance said as he glanced at his watch.

Wrapping one arm around Jeremy's back, he lifted his brother to his feet. They slowly crossed the room to the top of the staircase. Jeremy grabbed the banister and adjusted his weight to lean on the wooden railing.

"Give me two minutes to change and turn off the lights," Chance said.

"Grab my bag in the corner of the ballroom?" Jeremy requested before he started hopping down the stairs, holding his left leg out in front of him.

His body screamed with each jolt, but he refused to give in. He hadn't given in so far, and he wouldn't do so now. Not with Chance here watching his every move. He refused to show weakness in front of his brother, though all he wanted to do was curl up and cry like a newborn. He reached the landing between the second and third floors and paused long enough to wipe the sweat from his face. He did a couple of one-legged deep knee bends to loosen up his right leg. Then he continued his descent.

Chance changed into his street clothes and hung his sweat soaked dance clothes on a hook to dry. He'd have to remember to bring some clean clothes the next time he came by. Stacy and Remi refused to dance with him when he smelled like an old gym locker. Reentering the main room, he picked up Jeremy's bag and flipped off the lights and stereo system. Then he raced down the stairs to make sure his brother had not somersaulted down the stairs.

Jeremy had made it to the first floor landing. Chance studied his brother in the dim light available from the parking lot. He looked completely done in. His eyes were sunk deep into his skull. His complexion was gray. Chance settled on the step next to his head.

"It's over, isn't it?" he asked softly.

Jeremy opened his eyes to meet his brother's gaze. His eyes were bright with unshed tears. From physical or emotional pain, Chance wasn't sure.

"Yeah, I think so. I knew it was just a matter of time, but…"

"It's hard to admit that you're too old when you still feel like a kid inside," Chance said.

He still remembered the day he'd driven into Baltimore and joined the ranks auditioning for the Baltimore Ballet. He'd been twenty-five at the time, a good six to eight years older then everyone else present. With no professional credits to his name, the dance master called him aside and told him they wouldn't even consider him.

"You're too old for the chorus and too inexperienced for anything else. Give it up. I see you're a teacher. Send us your best and brightest students when they're sixteen, and we'll be happy to give them an audition." Handing him back his résumé, the man turned and headed to the stage.

Chance returned to the hotel room he'd rented near the theater and allowed himself an hour to mourn the end of his dream. Then he'd packed his bags and returned to Romney. His dream of dancing professionally trailed behind him in ashes. Since then, he'd concentrated on making Stacy and Remi happy. He still dreamed about dancing, but he only danced when there was no one to judge him.

"Yeah. It's hard to admit that the body can't keep up with the spirit," Jeremy said. He sat up with a groan. "Okay, big brother, help an old man to his car," he quipped.

❦

Remi opened the door of the mailbox slowly, half prepared for the box to explode in her face. Surely the post office wouldn't look at her picking up Dottie's mail as stealing. After all, Dottie was dead and no one had thought about the mail for almost a week. There might be bills that needed to be paid or letters that needed an answer.

Remi reached into the box and pulled out the stack of mail. Half of it was junk mail with only three bills. The rest was addressed "To the family of Dottie Applewhite." Remi blinked fast to keep from crying again. Every time she saw Dottie's name, she wanted to cry. As if she hadn't already cried enough tears to send the Potomac out of its banks.

Closing the box, she carried the mail to one of the counters and sorted it. She pulled out the junk mail and the sales flyers from Kendall's Grocery and Eckerd's Drug Store. No one would be interested in those.

"Remi? Remi Applewhite? How are you doing, honey?" A woman ducked out from behind the counter and appeared at Remi's elbow just as she tossed the junk mail in the trash.

"Hello, Miss Henrietta. I'm okay. Just came by to pick up Dottie's mail." Remi tried to smile at the woman who barely came up to her chin.

Henrietta Pearsall had worn the same uniform as long as Remi could remember. A silky white blouse with sleeves rolled into neat little folds just above her elbows. Her navy blue skirt stopped two inches below her knees, no matter what fashion dictated the proper length should be. A blue and white striped oversized smock substituted for the sweater she wore whenever she wasn't at the post office.

At seventy-five years of age, Henrietta had defied the government ten years earlier when they'd tried to retire her. No one else wanted the job, and she loved her work. It gave her a reason to get up in the morning, she told people. Besides, how else was she to know what was going on if she wasn't in the thick of it? Remi hoped that when she was as old as Dottie and Miss Henrietta, she would be just as active and happy.

"You going over to Dottie's place?" Miss Henrietta asked, peering over her gold rimmed half-glasses.

"Yes, ma'am."

"Good. Take this box to your Uncle Jeremy." Henrietta

hefted a white plastic U.S. Postal bin up onto the counter.

"All that's for Uncle Jeremy?" Remi's eyes widened at the stacks and stacks of letters bundled together with rubber bands.

"Yes, they've been arriving addressed General Delivery for the last two days. Hate to see what's going to arrive next week when people find out exactly where he's staying. Tell that uncle of yours if he's going to stay in town he needs to come by and see me. He has to either open a box or fill out paperwork so Dave can deliver to the house. I don't have room in the back for this much mail," Henrietta fussed.

"Yes, ma'am. I'll tell him," Remi said. She slipped Dottie's mail down the side of the bin. "I'll tell him to bring this box back, too."

"Thanks, honey. You're a treasure. Just like your grandma," Henrietta said. She patted Remi's shoulder while reaching into the pocket of her smock for her oversized linen handkerchief to wipe her eyes. "This whole town is going to miss Dottie. She was a very special lady."

"Yes, ma'am, she was. I'll see you, Miss Henrietta." Remi lifted the bin, staggering under the unexpected weight. How had this bird-like woman lifted it so easily?

Pushing her way out the front door, she wondered how she was ever going to carry the heavy box the six blocks to Dottie's house. "One step at a time," she told herself, remembering the advice her father had given her when she'd had to learn her first dance for a solo recital. "One step at a time, then move on."

By the time she'd walked a block and a half, she was ready to give in. Maybe she should have left Uncle Jeremy's mail at the post office for him to pick up.

"Hey Dancer, need a ride?"

Remi glanced over her shoulder just as the pickup truck

with the dull paint job and roaring engine pulled to a stop beside her.

"Hi T.J.," Remi returned. She kept walking, gritting her teeth against the weight of the box and the cramping in her upper arms.

"Climb in, I'll give you a ride." The tall blonde heartbreaker slowed the truck and rolled down Main Street, keeping pace with her.

"The last time you gave me a ride home, my dad grounded me for a week." As a sophmore, Remi wanted to be liked by the older kids, but T.J. had a reputation for being fast and loose. Remi wasn't sure she wanted to be friends with him, even though he did own a truck and was one of the handsomest seniors in school.

"Come on. I'll take you wherever you want to go. I won't even charge you," he teased as the truck rolled forward. Henry Millard honked behind him, wanting the truck to either move along or get off the road. "Come on Dancer, that box must be getting heavy."

"Oh, all right, I could use a ride to Dottie's house," she said. T.J. wouldn't care how many cars piled up behind him; he was determined to give her a ride. Because it was the middle of the afternoon and they were only going a few blocks, he couldn't do anything rash, like kidnap her for a picnic or a moonlit stroll down by Parson's Creek.

T.J. threw the truck into park and slid across the seat to open the door. With a groan, Remi lifted the box onto the seat. Sliding the box to the center of the bench seat, she climbed in.

He waited until she'd buckled her seatbelt before putting the gearshift into drive and pulling out. "That wasn't so hard, now was it?" he asked as he drove with one hand on the wheel and the other out the open window.

"No, but I don't need any trouble, so just drop me off at Dottie's, okay?" Remi kept one hand on the door handle and the other on the box to keep it from sliding off the plastic covered seat.

"Sure thing, Dancer." T.J. said. He floored the accelerator and then had to jam the brakes in order to turn into the driveway next to Dottie's house.

"Here you are, safe and sound, Dancer." He threw the gearshift into Park then shifted and looked at her. He smiled the smile that turned other young women into warm apple butter, but Remi didn't notice. She was busy opening her door and wrestling with the box that had separated them during the trip.

"Thanks for the ride, T.J. I'll see you," Remi said. Climbing down, she pulled the box out of the truck, then nudged the door close with one elbow.

"Yeah, I'll be seeing you, Dancer." T.J. put the truck into gear and hit the gas. He spewed gravel as he whipped out onto the road. He didn't bother to check traffic and almost ran over Wendell Montgomery in his thirty-year old Cadillac. The mistake embarrassed him, so he changed gears with a grinding clunk and squealed tires in an effort to get away.

Remi watched, confused for a moment. T.J. didn't stop or slow down. Shrugging, she climbed the porch steps. She put the bin on the ground and tried the back door. The knob turned under her hand so she opened it and dragged the bin through the door. Her arms and back were sore from carrying the heavy box, but she hadn't delivered the package yet.

"Dad? Uncle Jeremy? Anybody home?" she called as she lifted the bin and set it on the kitchen table.

"Yeah, honey. We're in Dottie's room," her father answered.

9

Remi stopped in the bedroom doorway when she saw that her father and uncle weren't alone. The third man was a stranger. The black bag at the foot of the bed and the pained looked on Jeremy's face told Remi he was a doctor. But Doctor Spencer was the only doctor who made house calls.

"As I've been telling you for the last two years, it's time to give up performing and look into a career that's not so stressful on that knee," the doctor said.

"Yeah, you've told me. And I haven't been listening. Well, now I am. What can we do about this?"

"No weight on it for a month. I'll schedule surgery to go in and look around. I think replacements will be the way to go. We'll have to see about the right one after we deal with this crisis." The doctor rummaged through his bag, finally coming up with a small pad. He scribbled on several sheets, tearing off one at a time and handing them to Chance. "A painkiller and an anti-inflammatory to help with the swelling. Here's one for a pair of crutches and one for a knee brace. If you can't get them locally, call my office and I'll send everything you need." He looked from Chance to Remi.

"You're going to have your hands full keeping him off his feet for a month. Good luck." With that, the doctor snapped his little black bag shut and left.

"Who was that?" Remi asked to break the tension between the two men.

"Dr. Brenton Michaels from New York. Your father called and squealed on me," Jeremy grumbled.

He flipped the blanket over his knee. No reason to scare Remi. The sight of his knee sent shivers down his spine.

"I'll go get these filled." Chance hoped Gary Armwood at Eckerd's would have everything they needed. "Can you stay here for awhile and be your uncle's legs?"

"Sure, Dad. Mom said she'd meet me at the Rail for dinner about six."

"Thanks, honey. Don't let him get out of that bed, and don't play poker with him. He cheats." Chance ignored Jeremy's grumbling as he gave Remi instructions. Then he left and the two dancers were alone.

"So what brings you by this afternoon, sweet Remi?"

"I went by the post office and picked up Dottie's mail." Remi settled on the straight-backed chair right next to the bedroom door.

"Is Miss Henrietta still postmistress?" Jeremy shifted to lie on his side. He was so bored of being in this room that any distraction was a blessing.

"She says they're going to have to carry her out feet first. She had a bunch of mail for you. I brought it along with Dottie's," Remi hopped from the chair and raced to the kitchen. She carried the bin back to the bedroom and set it on the floor by the bed.

"Miss Henrietta also said to tell you that if you're going to be staying in town, you need to make arrangements for them to deliver the mail."

"I wonder if she'd let me set something up by phone since it doesn't look like I'll be going anywhere for awhile," Jeremy said. He watched Remi shift and wiggle in her chair. Curiosity was attacking her as she sat next to the box of mail. It was as if Christmas had come but she was being denied the opportunity to open her gifts.

"You want a job?" he asked.

"Mom and Dad say I'm too young to have a job," Remi replied. She never took her eyes off the box of letters.

"Well, we don't have to tell them about it, do we?"

"What's the job?"

"I need an assistant while I'm laid up. Someone who can run errands, mail letters, stuff like that. Think you might be interested?"

"Yeah, sure, but what about school and stuff?"

"School comes first, then dancing. You can help me out on the weekends or whenever you have some free time," Jeremy said. He tried to sound casual as he made the offer, but this was the answer to his problem. He wanted to spend time with this blonde angel, this next generation of Applewhite dancers.

Remi was quiet for so long he was certain she would turn him down.

"I'll pay you. Cash. Ten dollars an hour."

"Ten dollars an hour? That's too much," Remi protested.

"Not if we were in New York. Since I'm the boss, you'll just have to accept what I want to pay. Okay?"

"Yes, sir," Remi said. She took a deep breath as she added up the money she could make and the hours she could spend here with her uncle. "When do I start?" she asked.

"You already did. Let's sort this mail and see about answering some of it." Jeremy waved his hand over the post office bin.

Remi nodded, picked up the first bundle of letters and pulled off the rubber bands holding it together. Shifting her chair so it was next to the bed, they began sorting the letters into piles of bills to be paid, letters he would answer personally, letters to be sent to Harry, his business manager, and junk mail to be thrown away.

"What about the ones that smell?" Remi asked, holding out an envelope that smelled strongly of perfume.

"They go to Harry. None of my friends would send a perfumed letter. Most of my friends don't write, anyway. They pick up the phone and call," Jeremy said, making a face. "Letters like that are from women who try too hard. Remember that so you won't send smelly letters to strangers."

"Okay, but what if someone sends me a smelly letter?" Remi tossed the letter onto the growing pile to be forwarded to Harry.

"Do what Harry's going to do for me. Send them a form letter thanking them for their kind thoughts and words. And don't forget to enclose an autographed picture. Fans can be your best friends or your worst enemies, depending on how you treat them. Always remember, you wouldn't be a star if it weren't for people who send smelly letters."

Remi giggled.

As she sorted the letters, handing only a few to her uncle, Remi came across a familiar handwriting. It was the letter she'd sent her uncle a few days before Dottie's death. Embarrassed, she slid it into the middle of the stack of junk mail. No need for him to see it now; he wasn't going anywhere any time soon.

"Uncle Jeremy, do you think a dancer should go to a performing arts high school to become a professional?" Remi asked her question carefully, trying hard to keep her voice casual, but failing miserably.

When he didn't answer her right away, she looked at him. She met his studious stare and forced herself not to look away. If she wanted to make her dream come true, she needed to be strong and courageous, not shy.

Finally Jeremy dropped his gaze to the letter in his hand. He cleared his throat and said, "I think that a dancer should concentrate on dancing whenever she can, wherever she is. She should take part in every performance she can get into and build up her résumé. Dancing in a performing arts high school might be nice, but you might lose something very important along the way. Stay here, study hard, dance and dance and dance, and enjoy life."

Chance came into the room just then. "They didn't have the right size crutches, but they're calling around and should get a pair in tomorrow. I did get your pills and the knee brace,"

"Thanks for the help, Remi. I'll call Henrietta in the morning about the mail," Jeremy said.

"Sure thing, Uncle Jeremy. I'll see you tomorrow." Remi waved as Chance shooed her from the room.

"You're late meeting your mom," Chance observed.

"Dottie's mail is on the kitchen table, along with some sympathy cards. See you tomorrow, Dad," Remi called as she raced through the kitchen.

"Yeah, tomorrow," Chance called after her. He wasn't looking forward to going back inside and facing his brother. But Jeremy needed someone to take care of him, and he was elected by default.

☙

Remi slid into the booth opposite her mother and murmured, "Sorry I'm late. I was keeping an eye on Uncle Jeremy while Dad went to Eckerd's for the doctor."

"Is something wrong with Jeremy?" Stacy asked.

"He messed up his knee. A specialist came all the way from New York City to see him. The doctor said he was going to have to give up dancing," Remi said. She squinted to read the blackboard across the room. "I'll be right back, Mom. I want to see what the specials are."

"They're the same as last week, sweetheart," Stacy said to the girl's back as the teenager slipped out of the booth.

Remi crossed to the blackboard, returning greetings to Ingrid and Katie, the two waitresses, as well as several customers. She paused in front of the board just long enough to read the Friday night specials: meatloaf, grilled chicken, and chili. Wrinkling her nose, she turned to head back to the table. When would her father ever change the specials?

"Hi, Remi," Toby North said softly in her ear.

"Toby, hi!" Remi jumped in surprise, but turned and smiled as she recovered from her fright. Toby North was top of the class in math and would rather work on his notebook computer than play sports. Tonight he was wearing an apron over his T-shirt and jeans. He was carrying a tray of dirty dishes. "When did you start working for my dad?" Remi asked.

"Last week. I need to save for college, and your dad needed a busboy on the weekends." Toby blushed and dropped his gaze to the floor.

At sixteen, Toby was still growing into himself. He still fumbled and bumbled as he learned to adjust to the added inches he'd grown in the least six months.

"Uh, I was wondering if you'd like to go out with me some time?" Toby said. He'd practiced the words a thousand times in his head but never dared to say them out loud. From the expression on her face, he'd actually spoken them so she could hear him.

Remi looked startled before her smile widened. "I'd like that. But I'll have to check with my mom." Remi flicked her glance to the last booth where her mother was sitting. Stacy was staring at her with one eyebrow cocked much higher than the other was. "I gotta go, Toby. Call me, okay?"

"Yeah, sure," Toby replied. He was stunned by Remi's positive response.

Remi scurried back to her mother. She deftly avoided the three couples circling the center of the room on what was jokingly called a dance floor.

"Katie, I'll have the grilled veggie platter, please," Remi said as she slid into the booth.

"Sure thing, Remi. You got something going on with Toby?" Katie said. She pocketed her order pad, having already recorded Remi's order before the girl's arrival. Every Friday night it was the same routine. The girl studied the specials and then ordered the grilled vegetable platter. Her father had added the dish to the menu just for her and had been surprised when it became popular with his other customers.

"Not exactly. But he did ask if I'd go out with him sometime," Remi gushed, her cheeks blossoming with color.

"That's great, honey. He's a hard worker, that one. With his mama raising him, I'm sure he knows the proper way to treat a lady." Katie said. She cocked an eyebrow in Stacy's direction. "All you got to do is convince your mom that Toby's nothing like T.J."

Remi studied her mother's face. She was staring at her like she'd grown another head. Or was she even seeing her? She looked like she was deep in thought.

"Mom?" Remi said once Katie moved on.

Stacy blinked and her daughter came back into focus. Her

mind had traveled back in time. She'd been a year older than Remi when a boy had asked her out for the first time. Chance had asked her to a school dance. She'd turned him down because her mother said he was too wild for her. He'd only been two years older than Stacy, but he had been the wild Applewhite brother. A couple of months later Jeremy asked her to the Christmas formal. Her mother had approved, saying Jeremy seemed steady.

It took a while before Stacy realized that she'd dated the wrong brother. As time went on, Chance had become the steady one while Jeremy ran wild, shying away from responsibility and maturity. Though he wore his hair too long, had a gold hoop in his right ear, and roared around town on his motorcycle, Chance had grown into a successful businessman. He also proved to be a wonderful husband and father.

"Mom?"

Blinking, Stacy focused on her daughter. "Yes, sweetie?"

"Would it be okay if I went out with Toby?"

"We'll talk about it when he asks you out on an real date, okay?"

"Yeah, okay," Remi said. She couldn't keep from radiating her happiness, especially when Toby passed by and winked at her.

"Mom, are you and Dad going to get a divorce?" Remi asked in the short time between Toby clearing their plates and Katie bringing desert.

Stacy blinked and focused on her daughter. "I hope not, honey. I sure hope not."

"Why did he move to Dottie's house?"

"We had a fight and did something we never did before. We went to sleep without solving the problem," Stacy said.

"I think you guys need to talk," Remi said after mulling over her mother's answer.

꙳

Chance stood watching Jeremy sleep and made a decision. He was going to intrude on Mother-Daughter Night. Between painkillers and exhaustion, Jeremy would sleep until morning. He didn't need to hang around just to watch the man breathe.

He might not have married Stacy for undying love, but it had bloomed. Now all he felt was a consuming love for her and fear that he would lose everyone if he didn't fix things right now, tonight.

He changed into a pair of black jeans and the blue polo Stacy had bought him because it matched his eyes. After pulling on his boots, he took the time to shave and splash on the cologne Stacy had brought the day of the funeral. Combing his hair, he tried to recall the last time he'd taken special care with his appearance for Stacy. He frowned when he couldn't remember. He'd been letting himself go.

"That ends now," he admonished his reflection. "This separation is crap and it's going to end, too." Running fingers through his curly black hair, he took a deep breath. "Go get her, Bubba."

He walked the handful of blocks to the restaurant. "Stacy darlin', I'm sorry. I don't know what I was thinking," he said softly.

"Hell, I don't even remember what the fight was about. Why am I apologizing?"

"Because you're miserable and you love her," he answered himself.

Pulling open the door to the Brass Rail, his eyes went to the booth in the back. The family traditionally used the last booth to the right whenever they gathered. Otherwise the staff hung out there. He slowed as he approached the table, straining to hear the conversation between the two women he loved more than anything else in the world.

"I think you guys need to talk," Remi said as she played with her pie. It was just the opening Chance needed.

"I agree wholeheartedly," he said. He slid into the booth beside Stacy. It was a spur of the moment action he hoped would work. "We do need to talk. About a lot of things." He looked at Stacy, reading surprise, heartache, and longing in her warm brown eyes.

"Yes, we do," Stacy said. She met Chance's gaze and smiled in welcome.

"I'll walk back to Dottie's house and stay there tonight. That way someone will be with Uncle Jeremy, and you can have some privacy," Remi said. She pushed out of the booth and disappeared before either parent could focus enough to understand her words.

10

Stacy's stomach quivered and rolled. It had been a long time since she'd seen that hungry glow in her husband's eyes. "I'm sorry we fought," she said softly. She lifted one hand to her husband's cheek, her palm fitting over his jaw. She stroked the razor smooth skin there and wanted him. Right here. Right now.

All thoughts of talking and working out the problems they faced shattered in the face of this hunger. All she wanted was to take him home and prove that the love had not lessened between them.

"Me, too," he whispered.

He leaned closer, brushing his lips over her cheek, then nuzzling the sensitive spot underneath her ear.

"Want to go home and make up?" Stacy whispered. She angled her neck just enough to allow him free access. His touch to that spot sent shards of want to her heart and other places lower in her body.

"Can you hold on long enough to get to the house?"

"I'll try to control myself," she said, "but you'd better drive." She pulled the keys from her purse and slipped them into his hand.

❦

Remi left the restaurant and turned toward Dottie's house. As Remi walked down Main Street, she felt like the last person alive in town. The shops and offices closed by six o'clock, except for the Gas 'N Go, the Brass Rail, and Eckerd's. Romney was a dying town. Every spring, just after the high school graduation, there was a mass exodus of those who'd made it. Few returned in the fall, having spent the summer traveling, looking for somewhere else that felt like home. Most moved away, settling in far off places. They only returned for short periods during the winter holidays or the summer festival season.

Remi wasn't sure if she'd make it to graduation here. She had sent inquiries to the New York High School for the Performing Arts as well as similar schools in Philadelphia, Washington, D.C., and Chicago. She wanted to go further in her dancing than just performing in recitals and talent contests and the Founder's Day Extravaganza. She wanted to follow Uncle Jeremy into the professional world of dance.

A shiver ran up Remi's spine. The back of her neck tingled. Her stomach knotted like it did every time she went on stage. Long ago she'd given up trying to eat before a performance. Her mother had carried cans of Carnation Instant Breakfast with her instead. Remi needed to eat as soon as she stepped offstage. The canned drink was enough to keep her from starving until the family reached the Brass Rail, where a real meal waited.

Nerves jangling, she quickened her pace, then tripped on the uneven sidewalk in front of the library. Quick stepping kept her from falling to the ground.

Crossing the street, she started to jog down the middle of Main Street. She could see Dottie's house up ahead. The front porch light was glowing like a beacon.

Remi's foot slid when she hit a patch of fresh gravel. The challenge to her balance sent her already-pounding heartbeat another notch higher. Instead of slowing, she kicked into high gear and ran for all she was worth. When she reached the Smith's yard next door to Dottie's house, she swerved and headed across the grass between the houses. The only sounds she could hear were her heartbeat and labored breathing.

She didn't stop until she'd climbed the steps to the porch, entered the back door, and locked it. She turned around and collapsed against the door. She panted with fear and the exertion of running.

It took two minutes to relax her body and slow her breathing. Her hands trembled when she reached to push her hair out of her face.

She was tempted to call the Brass Rail and talk to her dad. If she did that, her parents wouldn't talk. If they didn't talk, they'd never get back together, and that would suck!

Remi turned on the kitchen light, then the lights in the living room. She slipped into Jeremy's room and eased into the hard wooden chair by the bed.

He snored softly, his breath rhythmically soughing in and out. He'd kicked off his covers and looked cold, so Remi stood and pulled the covers over him, tucking him in. Her parents used to do the same thing for her not too many years ago. Brushing the hair back from his forehead, she whispered, "Good night, Uncle Jeremy."

After making sure all the windows and doors were locked, she retreated upstairs. Moving across the room in the dark, she found her dad's suitcase and pulled out one of his T-shirts. She took off her clothes and slipped on her father's shirt.

She pulled back the covers and slipped into bed, curling into a ball. She stared out the window by the bed before closing her eyes, snuggling down into the pillow and willing herself to sleep.

∼⌒

The crash woke her, but it was the thud and cursing that had Remi jumping from the bed and racing downstairs.

"Uncle Jeremy?" she called when she reached the bottom step.

"Where's Chance?" Jeremy grumbled.

"He and Mom are at home, hopefully making up. Are you okay?" Remi crossed to the open bathroom door where she could see her uncle's foot. It was bare. Thankfully, she didn't see any blood. She hated the sight of blood, whether it was her own or someone else's.

"I'm okay, but the lamp that was next to Dottie's bed is history. And I really could use your dad to help me in here." The foot disappeared.

Remi stepped closer so she could see all the way into the tiny bathroom. Jeremy was lying with his head next to the commode, pushing his upper body up while the rest of him remained flat on the floor. He arched his back and looked at the ceiling, stretching all the muscles down the front of his torso.

"Can I help?" she asked. Her uncle rolled over then sat up. He wasn't smiling. He looked sore and uncomfortable.

"How strong are you?" He held up both hands as he bent his good leg and braced the foot on the floor.

"Strong enough," Remi said. She grabbed his hands, planted her feet, and pulled. It took all her strength, but in a few seconds he was balanced on his one good leg, holding the other off the floor in front of him.

"Thanks, honey. I wasn't sure what I was going to do, other than make a mess." Jeremy grabbed the sink for balance. He smiled when Remi's cheeks bloomed with youthful embarrassment. "Could you do me a favor and put on a pot of coffee? My caffeine level is about a quart low."

Remi nodded and turned away. Her whole body blushed with shyness.

After setting up the coffeemaker and turning it on, she returned upstairs. She pulled on the clothes she'd worn the day before, then made the bed. Noting the pile of clothes in the corner, she decided it was time someone did laundry. She added her sleep-shirt to the pile, then carried the clothes downstairs. Once the laundry was started, she returned to the kitchen. She was starving.

"Remi?" Jeremy called from the bathroom.

"Yes, sir?"

"Can you come in here? I need some help." Jeremy hated asking anyone for assistance, but his strength was waning. His balance seemed to shift with each breath he took. His knee was throbbing and his stomach was growling. He was afraid that if he tried to hop to the kitchen, he'd end up on his butt again.

Remi hurried to his side. Even with one leg in the nylon and plastic brace, he was beautiful. She'd once read in *Dance World* magazine that he was the partner most dancers dreamed about. Only now he was hurt. If she understood the doctor correctly, he might never dance again. She'd always hoped to dance with her uncle on some stage, somewhere, someday.

"Lean on me," she said. She eased under his left arm, careful not to come into contact with his leg. One arm went around his waist as she tried to stand tall enough to be some help.

"Thanks, honey," Jeremy said. He tried to lean on her as little as possible, but he found her presence a welcome help.

Once they reached the kitchen, she settled him in the chair closest to the living room door. She turned a second chair so he could rest his leg on it. "You are truly a blessing," Jeremy praised her with a grin as she slid a mug of fresh, hot coffee across the table.

"She sure is," Chance said from the doorway.

Stacy followed him into the kitchen. They wore matching relaxed expressions. They each carried a paper bag full of groceries. Stacy and Remi unpacked the food while the men flipped through Dottie's mail. They opened cards, passed them back and forth, and wiped away the tears that came. Dottie would be missed by a lot of folks, as the cards demonstrated, but most of all by the four people in that kitchen.

In a few minutes, Remi set a bowl of scrambled eggs and cheese on the table. Stacy pulled a cookie sheet of browned English muffins from the oven. Conversation over breakfast was stilted as each family member concentrated on eating.

Finally, Remi laid down her fork and looked at her parents. "So are you guys going to get a divorce, or what?" She held her breath. She didn't want her parents to divorce. They had a great life together. Why did they want to mess it up by not being married any more?

"Or what," Chance answered after a long period of staring into his wife's eyes.

" 'Or what?' What does that mean?" Remi jumped up and circled the table in three skipping hops. She wrapped her arms around her father's neck and squeezed. Chance pulled her arm down from his throat so he could breathe.

"That means we've got to find your uncle a pair of crutches because I'm moving home," Chance said. He shifted uncomfortably as Remi's arm tightened again, this time in joyful excitement.

"That's great!" Remi squealed, finally releasing her father. She hugged her mother just as enthusiastically. "Isn't that great, Uncle Jeremy?"

"Yeah, great," Jeremy agreed after a long moment.

Remi didn't see that the smile on his face was forced. But he caught everyone's attention when he turned in his chair and slammed his leg into the table leg.

"Ouch! Damn!" The curse flew out before he could sensor himself.

"Uncle Jeremy! You owe the Pig a quarter," Remi scolded.

"The Pig?" Jeremy asked as he rubbed his leg.

"You remember Gus the Cuss Pig, don't you?" Chance asked with a chuckle.

"Gus the Cuss Pig? Is he still around? I figured he'd gone into retirement by the time you moved out," Jeremy said, smiling.

Gus the Cuss Pig had consumed more of his money than anything else had the year he'd turned fifteen. Dottie had not been impressed with the curse words peppering their language. She had produced an antique piggybank and instituted a nickel penalty for anyone caught cursing. The penalty was per word, not per curse. The boys liked to be inventive in their name calling, so Gus filled up fast. That was when the donation came into play. Dottie sat them down and explained that because the pig was a penalty, the best thing they could do was make a donation to one of the local charities. The boys agreed, and the fire station received the first donation from Gus the Cuss Pig.

"A quarter? It used to be a nickel."

"Inflation, Uncle Jeremy," Remi explained patiently.

Pulling a piece of paper toward him, he picked up a pen and wrote out an IOU to Gus. "Where is old Gus, anyway?" Jeremy asked as he looked around the kitchen. The special shelf where Gus resided during the boys' teenage years now held a pair of ceramic figurines.

"He lives at the restaurant now. Dottie brought him with her on her second visit and demanded that we put him into practice. She didn't like all the cursing going on in the kitchen. The customers liked the idea, so he found a new home. After all, I run a family restaurant," Chance explained.

"Do you still donate the proceeds to charity?"

"In one form or another. Gus donates his earnings to local charities or to families in town who've either been flooded out or who've had house fires," Stacy answered.

"It's been a great advertising tool for the restaurant," Chance added. "Every time Gus makes a donation, the paper runs a story about Gus the Cuss Pig and how he came into being, along with the background on his latest choice of charities. Which leads to a lot of swearing at the restaurant in order to fill Gus again."

"Well, since I don't have any pockets, you'll just have to hold onto my IOU. Okay, Remi?" Jeremy said as he slid the paper across the table toward his niece.

"I guess it will have to do since you don't have a quarter." Remi slipped the paper into her pocket. "Do you want me to help you back to bed now?"

"I guess. Then you can run an errand or two for me, if it's okay with your parents." Jeremy allowed the girl to help him stand up.

"Sure," Remi said. She wrapped one arm around his waist and prepared for his weight. In two minutes they were out of the kitchen and across the living room to Dottie's room.

"They're good for each other," Stacy pointed out gently.

"Yeah, that's what scares me," Chance muttered into his coffee mug. Pushing from his chair, he rose. "I'm going to swing by the drugstore and see if Gary has those crutches yet." He kissed his wife, then kissed her again, the hunger that had been with him since the night before rising again.

"Go away, you horny old man. I've got to get this house cleaned up and then get to the studio for classes."

11

For the first time in weeks, Chance felt blessed. Stacy held his hand, and his daughter and brother followed just behind as they stepped onto the church grounds and headed for services on Sunday. It was a morning for thanking God for all He'd done. Though Dottie's passing wasn't something to cheer about, he was even thankful that she was at peace. His grandmother had been ready to make the journey to the next life. He heard gasps and then whispers, the loudest coming from the clutch of gossips that gathered each Sunday to compare stories and trade secrets.

"Ladies," he said. He nodded with a smile while tightening his grip on Stacy's hand.

The six ladies in their Sunday dresses and matching accessories gawked as the Applewhite family passed. Chance knew they'd expected Stacy and Remi, but not the Applewhite brothers.

"Be nice," Stacy murmured. "Some of these ladies were Dottie's oldest friends." Turning to the ladies, she smiled and said, "Good morning. Lovely weather today."

"Chance, Stacy. So nice to see you together…I mean here," Henrietta Pearsall sputtered as the others murmured their good mornings.

"Nice to be here, Miz Henrietta," Chance drawled lazily.

He released Stacy's hand and wrapped his arm around her shoulder. He pulled her closer so their sides meshed. He never changed his ambling pace, so the ladies of the Gossip League had to follow them down the sidewalk or move on to someone else. With a "Good morning" to Jeremy and Remi, the ladies returned to their circle and their hushed gossiping.

Chance chuckled and looked over his shoulder at Jeremy. "Hopefully, that will keep the spotlight off you. At least until after the service. By then the mothers of all the eligible young women in town will be laying in wait for you."

"So what do I do? I can't outrun them," Jeremy said. He grew pale at the idea of being ambushed by marriage-minded mothers with man-hungry daughters in tow.

The crutches were a godsend, but there was no way he could escape the women of Romney. He couldn't be mean to them. He was known the world over for making time for anyone who asked. People made up audiences and without them, he'd be the attendant at the Gas 'N Go just north of town.

"Tell them your leg's hurting and you need to get home," Stacy offered with a smile. "That should get you out of the lunch invitations."

"By suppertime you'll be swimming in chocolate cake, apple pie, and casseroles," Chance said.

"Don't worry, Uncle Jeremy. I'll protect you," Remi offered.

"Thanks, honey, but I think I can defend myself. I just have to figure out how," Jeremy said. He smiled at the girl who would willingly throw herself in front of a town full of determined mamas to save her bachelor uncle.

❧

After the benediction, Jeremy eased back onto the bench seat in the middle of the church. He relaxed as those around him gathered their belongings and began the slow procession toward the back of the church. He planned to sit and wait until everyone was gone. He didn't want to knock anyone over with his crutches.

Closing his eyes, he prayed, asking for guidance in closing out his past and facing the uncertainty of his future. When he opened his eyes, he was almost alone. Stacy sat beside him, patiently waiting for him to finish.

"Ready?" she asked.

"Yeah, I guess. What happened to Chance and Remi?" Jeremy pushed to his feet and hopped toward the center aisle, dragging his crutches behind him.

"They went to bring the car around. That way you can make a faster getaway. You know, before you break every female heart in town," Stacy teased gently.

"Tell me something," Jeremy said. This was the best place to ask the question that had been eating at the back of his brain. Stacy would never lie to him, but to be on the safe side, he'd ask now while standing in the middle of holy ground.

"What?"

"Are you happy? With Chance, I mean."

"Yes, I'm happy. He's been solid and loving and good to me."

"Is Remi mine?"

Stacy froze for a moment, growing pale under her barely-there makeup. Swallowing hard, she spoke so softly that Jeremy had to strain to hear, "I found out the week before graduation. She's from your seed, but she's Chance's daughter. He raised her, he loved her, and he has been her father for sixteen years." Blinking back tears, she asked, "What are you going to do?"

Jeremy remained silent for a full minute. "Nothing. She

is Chance's daughter. It would only hurt her if I demanded that she leave everything to come to me. I tried that with her mother, and look where it got me. I just needed to know. I want to be a part of her life, even if only as Uncle Jeremy." Jeremy turned and slowly headed to the back of the church. "Thanks for telling me. Will you tell me about her growing up sometime? Catch me up on her life and yours?"

"Yes," she answered, just before they stepped onto the church's porch. "Tomorrow at the studio. Ten o'clock."

Jeremy nodded, then took the step into the sunlight so everyone could see him. The crowd that remained was almost scary it was so large, but he'd dealt with larger crowds before. Only in the past, they hadn't been people he knew. He didn't want to offend anyone by rushing to the car that Chance had parked only twenty-five feet away.

"What do I do?" Jeremy asked. He looked at Stacy, his eyes wide.

"Keep moving. And remember, you need to get home and rest," Stacy said. She smiled, amazed at this side of Jeremy. She'd never seen him afraid of anything before. But obviously this hometown crowd of people who loved him scared him to death.

❧

By the time the sun sank behind the mountain that afternoon, Jeremy was ready to climb in his car and, bad knee be damned, drive far, far away—somewhere people didn't know him, his family, and his vulnerabilities. Someplace that didn't have twenty-two young single women with mamas. In the last three hours, each and every one had stopped by with food. The concern had been touching, but by the time the last four finally left the yard, Jeremy was beyond tired.

The first pair rang the bell at one o'clock and waited for him to answer the door. Jeremy moved to the back porch to watch the parade for the next four hours. And what a parade it had been. Cars lined the street and women marched in and out of the kitchen. They *tsk-tsked* his brace and crutches and asked in the same concerned tone, "Does it hurt very badly? Will this affect your career? Are you thinking of staying in town for long?"

He didn't know the answers about his career and his future, so he smiled politely and ignored the questions. Now, as mamas all over town called their children for dinner, Jeremy was finally able to relax. Ella Simpkins and her mother had been the last. They'd spent ten minutes putting a vegetable medley casserole on the stove. No doubt they'd checked the cupboards for dust, but there was none to be found. The other women had beaten them to it. As soon as their truck left the driveway, Jeremy hopped into the kitchen and pulled the last can of beer from the back of the refrigerator. Returning to the porch, he settled into Dottie's rocker. He propped his leg up on the wooden box he'd found earlier and popped the top off the beer.

Tipping back the can, he consumed half the contents. Lowering the can, he smiled as a protracted, rattly burp escaped into the otherwise quiet night air. With fall approaching, even the crickets and tree frogs had grown silent.

"Well, that was certainly impressive," Chance commented as he climbed the three steps to the porch.

"Thank you. I do try to impress," Jeremy replied. He used his good leg to set the rocker in motion. "You with the sobriety police?"

"Nah. Remi had a church group outing and needed a ride out to the fairgrounds. Stacy ordered me to stop by here and make sure you survived the afternoon," Chance said. He eased onto the swing and set it in a motion that matched his brother's rocking. "Besides, this is a good time to talk."

"Oh?" Jeremy asked. "What's the subject?"

"The past, the present, the future. Dottie's will." Chance shifted. He didn't want this conversation. It was bound to turn painful or ugly or both.

Jeremy had guessed at Remi's paternity and had agreed not to steal her. But Remi's hero worship pained Chance, though he couldn't blame her. Jeremy was a world famous dancer. All her life, Remi had dreamed about being on the stage, no matter how much Chance tried to dissuade her. He knew from personal experience that heartache waited out there.

"All that, huh? Then we're going to need dinner and I happen to have enough food to keep a small country fat and happy," Jeremy said. He stood and hobbled toward the kitchen.

He headed straight for the refrigerator. "What's your pleasure, ham, beef, or chicken?"

"Sit down before you fall and really hurt yourself. I'll fetch the food."

"Okay, fine. Be a worrywart." Jeremy said as he hopped to the nearest chair and sat down.

"I just don't want to eat off this floor. It hasn't been mopped since Dottie's been gone," Chance said.

"Yes, it has. Bachelorette number twelve and her mother cleaned the kitchen. Number eight did the bathroom, and fourteen vacuumed while her mother dusted. Six and ten changed the sheets on the beds, and fifteen folded the laundry that four got started. I wish I'd had neighbors like this in New York. It would have saved me from having to hire a cleaning service."

Chance placed the cold platters from the refrigerator on the table.

The brothers ate, not talking, not looking at one another. They ate generous helpings from each of the dishes.

"You've got to take some of this stuff home with you," Jeremy said after eating his fill. "Otherwise, I'll be as big as a house by the end of the week. Especially since I can't dance off all these calories."

"I'll take these dishes we started on, but you'll have to write the thank you notes," Chance said.

Picking up their empty plates, he rinsed and stacked them in the sink. He put the food away. Only when the kitchen was clean did he look at his brother.

"I love her," he said. "I love Remi like she's my own daughter. Hell, she is my daughter. I've been there for her and Stacy since before her heartbeat sounded in Stacy's belly. I don't want to lose them." Chance said. His eyes filled with tears, but he blinked fast to keep them from falling.

"I know you love them." Jeremy leaned forward, folding his hands on top of the table. "You do love Stacy don't you?"

Chance was stilled by the question. With a deep breath, he made the hardest confession of his life. "Yes, I love Stacy. I know she was your girlfriend, but she's the other half of my soul. The last couple of weeks we've been apart have been hell. I don't even remember why we fought.

"I married her because of the baby, but I never resented you for leaving. You didn't know about the baby. Your life, your career was out there, beyond the mountains. In fact, I've thanked you every day for the gift you unknowingly left behind."

"But you gave up your own dancing career..." Jeremy stopped trying to hide his tears.

"I love to dance, but I'm happy here running the Brass Rail and teaching," he said. He wiped his cheeks before continuing. "I've never had the inner drive you did. I wanted too many other things…"

"Like a family," Jeremy broke in. "But why didn't anybody contact me about the baby?"

Chance paused before swallowing hard. "We tried, but you'd moved several times before we finally found you. Remi was six months old when Dottie finally tracked down someone who claimed to know you. She kept in contact with your agent until you finally got in touch with her. She never told anyone she'd heard from you until the very end. The day before she died she told me where your number was. Only the phone had been disconnected and your agent refused to take my call."

"God, I wish I'd decided to come home a month earlier, a year earlier, a decade earlier," Jeremy admitted softly.

"Why did you come home? What is going on with you?" Chance asked.

Jeremy raised his beer and drank deeply, stalling so he could come up with an answer.

Why had he come home? To admit failure? Or to come to terms with the past? He felt so relaxed that he spoke without really thinking. "To tell the truth, I don't know myself. When I got in the car after my last meeting, it felt right to come home." His words ran together as the beer addled his brain.

"My career as a dancer is over," he said. He grimaced when he shifted in his chair. "Dancing, performing has been my life for seventeen years. Now that my career is over, I don't know who I am or what I'm supposed to do." The soul-baring confession was whispered hoarsely. "What am I supposed to do now?"

Jeremy leaned forward, slumping over the table. The painkiller he'd taken after the bachelorettes and their mothers had left relaxed him into unconsciousness.

Chance was stunned by his brother's blunt honesty. His response was the one Dottie had used when the brothers asked her what they should do with their lives. "Anything you want, my boy. Anything you want."

Jeremy didn't hear him. He was snoring softly, lost in his dreams. Chance half carried him to the bedroom, stripped him and put him to bed. Just as he tucked Jeremy in, the phone rang, shrilly splitting the silence.

"Hello?" Jeremy murmured. He rolled over and pulled the pillow over his head when the phone rang a second time.

Chance grabbed the phone and carried it to the living room, picking it up as it rang a third time. "Hello?"

"Chance? Is Remi with you?" Stacy asked, sounding more perturbed than scared.

"Why would she be here? Isn't she home from the picnic yet?"

"No, and I'm getting worried."

"I'll run out to the picnic grounds on my way home." Chance clamped the phone between his cheek and shoulder as he returned to the kitchen. He set up the coffeemaker, then pulled Dottie's picnic basket from the shelf in the closet and packed up the salads and casseroles he told Jeremy he'd take home with him.

"Are things between you and Jeremy okay?" Stacy asked.

"It's gonna take some time. But I think we'll be okay. I'll see you in about twenty minutes, okay?"

"Okay. Love you."

"Love you too, darlin'." As Chance climbed into his truck, his mind shifted from brother mode to father mode. Where was his daughter and what was she up to?

~⌒

The red, white, and blue lights flashing on the police cruiser made Chance pull over and park. A knot formed in his gut as he climbed from his car. He slowly approached a group of people standing by the side of the road. The mountain was steep here, the drop a forty-five-degree angle down to the Potomac River.

The sheriff was talking to two young men. Two young women huddled together nearby. He recognized T.J. Frederickson whose paper white skin gave away his shock. He didn't know the other boy, but he didn't appear happy with whatever the sheriff said. The boys looked as if they'd exchanged blows at some point. As he approached, one of the girls ran toward him.

"Daddy!" she cried.

Chance caught her as she threw herself at him. "Are you all right?" He hugged her then set her back on her feet and looked her over. She was shaking and had been crying.

"They're all okay, which is amazing, considering…" the sheriff said.

"Considering?" Chance looked from the sheriff to Remi. She wouldn't meet his eyes, so he turned back to the sheriff.

"Considering those two fools decided to race down the mountain. Seems they had an argument at the picnic and decided to settle it on the road." The sheriff closed his note-book. "These kids are lucky they're alive."

Chance pulled Remi close again. Wrapping his arms around her, he said a silent prayer as she burst into tears.

"I'm sorry, Daddy. If I'd have known this was going to happen I would have ridden home with Mrs. Leonard," she sobbed.

"It's okay, baby. Sheriff, are you finished with Remi? I'd like to take her home."

The sheriff frowned at Remi and said, "I don't want to see you again, unless it's onstage at the high school. All right?"

"Yes, sir," Remi said. She wiped her eyes and sniffed back the last of her tears.

"Okay, honey, let's go." Chance said.

"Can we take Holly home, too?" Remi asked.

12

The girls were quiet on the drive back to town. At Holly's house, Chance pulled up and parked. Before anyone could move, Holly's parents emerged from the house and raced across the yard.

"Are you okay?" her father demanded as soon as she opened the door.

"I'm fine," Holly murmured. She collapsed into her mother's arms.

Chance pulled her father aside and outlined what he knew. Then he climbed back into the truck and started for home.

Chance didn't say a word on the ten-minute drive from Holly's house to theirs. He couldn't begin to voice his swirling emotions. Fear, anger, and astonishment warred for dominance. Pulling into the driveway, he parked the truck, but didn't climb out immediately. Remi sat huddled against the door, finally finished with her tears. When he looked at her, she met his gaze steadily. Her tear-stained cheeks were pale in the moonlight.

"I don't know where to begin. I'm amazed that you'd do something so stupid. Getting in a car with another person on the road to self-destruction is a sure way to end up dead yourself. Thank God you came away with nothing more than a few bumps and bruises. You could have died." He tried to control his rage.

"I know. I'm sorry. I don't know why I did it exactly," Remi said. She wiped at her cheeks. "I'm sorry," she repeated. Unbuckling her seatbelt, she threw herself across the truck cab into his arms.

"That boy is trouble and I want you to stay away from him. I don't want him to ruin your life," Chance said. He held her tight. His tears fell into her hair as he held her. He rubbed her back and brushed her hair from her face. "You'll do stupid things again in the future. But for the next month, if you're not at school or with your mom at the studio, you'll be at the restaurant where I can keep an eye on you."

"What about Uncle Jeremy? He needs me," Remi said.

"Okay, you can be with your uncle, but if you're not at school, you'll be with one of us."

Remi wiped her cheeks again. "Yes, sir," she said softly.

It had been almost an hour since T.J. had peeled out of the picnic area's parking lot, but Remi's heart still pounded. A month of close supervision wouldn't be so bad. At least she could still talk on the phone and spend time with Uncle Jeremy.

She knew her father wanted an explanation, but she couldn't explain why she'd turned down Mrs. Leonard's offer of a ride and climbed into T.J.'s truck. He was trouble, but he made the race sound so exciting that she couldn't turn him down. It was a moment of teenage insanity, one of those moments when common sense got sidetracked by hormones.

Knowing she still had to face her mother, Remi followed her father to the front door of the house. As soon as she stepped inside, her mother grabbed her and hugged her.

"Are you okay?" she asked. She held Remi at arm's length and looked her up and down.

"Just sore," Remi replied. She stepped close and wrapped herself around her mother.

"Myra called and told me what happened. Don't you ever, ever ride with that Frederickson boy again! I thought we'd worked this out last summer," Stacy said. She blinked back tears of relief as she cuddled her daughter close.

Remi allowed the closeness for several moments. Finally, she pulled out of her mother's arms. "I've got to go take a shower," she said. She turned away and sniffed back tears that wouldn't stop. Wiping at her cheeks, she hurried from the room.

ॐ

Jeremy woke feeling like he'd slept for a week. He was stiff and sore and his mouth tasted like the inside of one of his old dance shoes. Blinking against the bright light, he tried to figure out what woke him. Then the answering machine clicked on and Stacy's voice sounded.

"Jeremy, it's 10:15. If you're still in bed, climb out and make yourself presentable. I'll be there in five minutes." Click.

Jeremy threw off the covers and groaned. His head pounded in protest against any movement. But the pain didn't stop him as he pulled sweatpants up over the brace. He hopped to the bathroom. He tested his leg while heading to the kitchen to start coffee.

"Thank you, brother," he said. All he had to do was turn on the coffeemaker. His stomach grumbling, he checked the refrigerator. Chance had taken several dishes home with him. The rest were stacked neatly in the refrigerator.

Jeremy straightened when the back door opened. "Good morning. Are you all right?" he asked. She looked pale.

"Morning. Are you okay? When you weren't at the studio, I got worried," Stacy said. She put down the stack of photo albums and notebooks she carried.

"I was reading in the Winchester paper that the Arts Council is putting together a Christmas production of *The Nutcracker*, and they're looking for young dancers," Jeremy said.

"I got a flyer about it last week. Are you going to contact them about dancing? Aren't you supposed to stay off that knee?"

"I wasn't thinking about me, I was thinking about Remi. She's perfect for Clara," Jeremy said. He spoke like a man who'd danced with a long line of young women not nearly as talented as his niece was.

"After last night, I'm not sure dancing *The Nutcracker* is appropriate. Not this year," Stacy said.

"What happened last night?" Jeremy asked. He served the cinnamon and raisin coffeecake one of the hopeful young ladies had left the day before.

"She got in some trouble last night and is grounded for a month. When she's not in school she has to be with one of us at all times."

"I am included in the us?" Jeremy asked.

"Yes," Stacy said. "Chance relented on that because she's worried about who will take care of you if she's not here to act as your assistant."

"What Chance doesn't know can't hurt him. Who knows, she might not even get the part," Jeremy said. He sipped his coffee as the idea took root in his brain and blossomed. "This is the chance she needs. It's a great part, and one most ballerinas start their careers with."

"I don't keep secrets from Chance. But if I didn't know about it, then I couldn't keep anything from him, could I?" Stacy replied.

"Right. I'll be the one keeping secrets," Jeremy said. He

grinned at the idea of Remi surprising her parents with such an accomplishment.

It would be a dream come true for Remi. It would give her a taste of what goes on behind the scenes of a production, the weeks of hard work that culminate in a handful of performances. The more he thought about it, the better he liked the idea. And if they happened to have a part for an old, broken down dancer as well, all the better. That way he could keep an eye on things.

"I need a key to the studio," he announced suddenly.

"A key? Why?" Stacy asked.

"So I can get in and rehearse. I think maybe I'll try out for the Christmas ballet in Winchester."

"But your knee—" Stacy started.

"My knee will be fine. I won't overdo anything, but I have to get back into dancing. My body is already rebelling. Everything I've worked for over last thirty years will be history soon enough. I can't get fat, too," Jeremy said.

Stacy thought a moment, then sighed. She knew how he felt. If she didn't dance for two days in a row, she felt itchy and cranky and out of sorts. He must be going crazy. "I'll get you a key, but my rule is that someone has to be there when you dance."

"Yes, mother," Jeremy replied with a grin.

꒰꒱

"So, kiddo, do you want to take a ride with me on Saturday?" Jeremy asked Remi as they sorted the mail Wednesday afternoon.

If he was careful and didn't try to fly, he could audition for a minor role in the Christmas production. But he was secondary. He wanted Remi to audition.

"Where to?" Remi asked. She flipped through the envelopes in front of her, quickly sorting them into the appropriate piles.

"I thought I'd go to Winchester. Want to go with me?"

"Sure, I guess. It'd be better than sitting around the restaurant with Dad," Remi said.

"I'll pick you up at noon at your house," Jeremy replied.

He'd decided to wait until Saturday to tell her exactly where they were going. Not used to children, he couldn't remember how well sixteen-year-olds could keep secrets. For now, this trip would remain a surprise. At least until they were sure Remi would be a part of the production.

"Uncle Jeremy?" Remi suddenly stopped and looked at him.

"Yes?"

"Are you going to live here now? I mean forever?" Remi asked, hoping his answer was that he would be returning to New York City soon. If so, she'd ask to go with him and attend LaGuardia High School.

Jeremy took a breath, relieved that her question wasn't about boys or sex or drugs. Then he thought about her question. It wasn't just about where he would live; it was about his life and what he was going to do with it.

"With my knee banged up, I can't dance. I'm getting too old to be performing like I have. I will live here at least until the new year. After that we'll see." The new year deadline would get them through rehearsals and performances of *The Nutcracker* if they were selected. It would also give his knee a chance to heal. He hoped knee replacements wouldn't be necessary, but he'd cross that bridge when he came to it.

"Oh, well. Do you think you could you get us invited to the White House Christmas tree lighting ceremony? I've seen it on television, but it would be so cool to be there to see it. And Washington is only a couple of hours away."

Jeremy grinned at her. "I'll make a couple calls and see what I can do," he replied. "Now, do I have any checks to write this week, or can I keep my money?"

$$\backsim$$

By Saturday, Jeremy could walk with a profound limp. He stretched in the living room to find out what his knee could and could not handle. Hopefully, his name and a quiet conversation with the director and choreographer would keep the secret of his bum knee out of the papers.

Well before noon he pulled into the driveway of Chance's mountainside home and was surprised to see both trucks in the driveway. Chance and Stacy were supposed to be at work. How was he going to explain their trip to Winchester? He tried several different excuses as he crossed the yard, using a single crutch to stabilize him. The front door opened as he slowly, painfully climbed the steps.

"Where the hell is your brace and the other crutch?" Chance demanded.

"In the car. I'm tired of being an invalid. The only way to overcome pain is to not give in to it. I've given my knee long enough to rest. Now it's time to put it back to work."

"Dr. Brenton said a month. It hasn't been a week and you're already disobeying doctor's orders," Chance said.

If you only knew, Jeremy thought as he entered the front door. "Nice place," he said.

"Thanks. I didn't have a thing to do with it except the manual labor. All the design stuff was Stacy's doing," Chance said. He closed the door, then leaned against it and crossed his arms. "So what are you doing in Winchester today?"

"I thought we'd go see a movie and maybe check out the mall. Don't worry Dad, I won't lose her or anything," Jeremy said.

"Yeah, but who's going to keep an eye on *you* is the question," Stacy remarked as she stepped into the room.

"That's why Remi's coming along. She's supposed to keep me out of trouble. Where is she, anyway?"

"In her room, primping no doubt." Stacy studied him closely.

"Can I talk to her for a minute before we go?" Jeremy asked.

"Sure, it's the last door down the hall." Stacy pointed across the living room.

"Thanks," Jeremy said. He moved down the hall casually, not stopping until he reached Remi's bedroom. He knocked on the closed door, waited for the "come in," and stepped inside. He glanced down the hall to see that no one had followed him.

"Hey, sweetie. You ready?"

"Yep, just brushing my hair, Uncle Jeremy."

"Do me a favor. Put your nicest rehearsal clothes and toe shoes in a bag."

"Why?" she asked as she moved to do as he requested.

"Because we're going to Winchester to work on a Christmas present for your parents. I'll tell you the rest in the car."

"It's *The Nutcracker* isn't it? We're going to try out for *The Nutcracker*!" Remi squealed in delight.

"Only if you can keep it a secret. I'm not sure your dad would consider this part of your punishment for your escapade last week, but if you want to be a ballerina, sometimes you have to bend the rules. And technically, I will be there keeping an eye on you, so we're not breaking his punishment."

Remi threw herself across the room, wrapping her arms around Jeremy's middle. "Thank you, Uncle Jeremy, thank you, thank you, thank you. Dad said I was too young to try out."

"Well, I don't think you're too young, or too old. I think you're just right." Jeremy returned her hug. "Now get ready. Auditions start at two, and you'll have to warm up once we get there."

Remi quickly filled her backpack with what she needed for the audition. She included the publicity shot with her résumé on the back that Dottie had fixed for her over the summer. After quick goodbyes to her parents, they were on their way. Neither spoke for long periods, both nervous and excited and scared of what was to come.

⌁

By the time they reached the sign announcing the Winchester city limits, the butterflies in Remi's stomach had morphed into dinosaurs doing a two-step in steel-toed boots.

She'd auditioned before, but this was different. She'd be alone. The only person she'd know would be Uncle Jeremy. He'd be busy talking with all the people who would recognize him. And everyone would recognize him.

She'd be on her own. But that's what she wanted, wasn't it? To prove to her parents she could handle herself as an adult. Sunday night had been a dumb thing to do. T.J. was bad news, and from now on she would stay far, far away from him.

But that was in the past. Today was the present. What would she dance for the audition? The piece she'd done for the school talent show last spring? Or the one she hadn't finished working on for the town's Christmas pageant?

"Uncle Jeremy, what should I dance?" Remi asked.

"How about the piece you showed me the other day? The one you haven't finished yet. That's a good piece. It shows your strengths and that you're more than just a pretty face." Jeremy said. He looked at her and was surprised to find her as pale as one of Dottie's white cotton sheets. Her fingers were knotted in her lap and her toes tapped rhythmically on the floorboards. "Don't worry. I'll be right there watching. You'll do just fine."

"But that piece isn't finished. I haven't figured out the ending," Remi whispered.

"At most auditions I've been to they stop you before you get too far into a piece. Explain that this is a work in progress, and dance what you have finished. If they let you finish, then stop, go into first position and wait for someone to speak. Don't say anything, just stand and wait. One sign of a professional is knowing when to speak and when to wait quietly."

Remi nodded, surprised to find that he'd driven to the Arts Council building without needing directions. The parking lot was half full, and people were slowly making their way to the front doors of the three story brick building. Remi swallowed hard and glanced at her watch: 1:05. She had an hour to change and warm up. And maybe throw up.

"Ready?" Jeremy asked. He reached into the back seat and pulled out a black nylon bag.

"I guess so," Remi agreed. She clutched her backpack to her quivering stomach. "I just hope I don't throw up onstage."

Once inside, Jeremy became a professional. "Okay, honey, you find a place and change your clothes, and I'll find a place for us to warm up," Jeremy said. "I'll meet you back here in five minutes."

"Better make it ten. Looks like there's a line for the bathroom," Remi said. She pointed toward the dozen or so girls lined up outside the women's room.

"Come now ladies, are you really so modest that only one of you can use the restroom at a time? You've all been given the same equipment. If you're shy, turn your back and face the wall while you change. And since there don't seem to be any men waiting around, you can use that room as well. You're dancers, be proud of your bodies," Jeremy said. The girls stared at him, wide-eyed and slack-jawed.

As soon as he'd had his say, he turned and began the search for a room to stretch and warm up in. Behind him, he heard one of the girls ask, "Who is that guy?" He turned a corner before Remi responded.

He found what he was looking for at the end of the hallway. A glass door led into a large, empty room. There was plenty of room for bending and stretching. There was even a freestanding barre tucked along one wall.

"Perfect," he murmured.

The only problem was that the door was locked. All the doors were locked. Turning around slowly, he checked out the hall.

13

"Who is that guy?" the tall, rail thin girl next to Remi asked. The girl's cheeks were pink with embarrassment as much as from shyness.

"Jeremy Applewhite. Marcie, don't you know anything about the world outside your school books?" another girl answered. She pushed through the handful of girls until she stood right in front of Remi. "How do *you* know Jeremy Applewhite?"

Remi swallowed before answering, "He's my uncle."

She wasn't sure why, but she didn't like this girl. Maybe it was her artificially colored ash blonde hair with dark roots. Or maybe it was the way she looked down her too skinny, turned up nose, her shrill voice half a tone away from whiney.

"I do know who Jeremy Applewhite is, Caitlyn. I just didn't recognize him offstage and out of costume. He's much cuter in person," Marcie defended herself. She turned to Remi and asked, "Want to share the bathroom with me?" She waved to the men's room that was still empty. None of the other girls seemed interested in that room. When the girl who was in the women's room finally emerged, three girls stepped inside before closing the door.

"Sure, come on," Remi said. She hitched her backpack higher on her shoulder, then stepped around Caitlyn and her two friends. After knocking loudly, she pushed open the door.

"If there's anyone in here, close your eyes because we're coming in," Remi called. She counted to five and entered the bathroom. It was a large room with a toilet in one corner and a sink in the other. There was plenty of room for them to change.

"You take that corner, and I'll take this one," Marcie said as she flipped the lock in the doorknob.

"Okay. If you want, I can help you with your hair." Remi dropped her backpack, then knelt beside it. It didn't take long to change, and she quickly pulled her hair up and secured it with the long pins the way her mother had taught her before her first recital. "You done yet?"

"Yes," Marcie replied hesitantly.

Remi turned and discovered that under the oversized clothes that made her look like a stick figure, Marcie had a beautiful body. She was long-limbed with subtle curves that spoke of coming womanhood.

"What's wrong, Marcie?" Remi stuffed her sneakers into her bag, then crossed to the other girl.

"I don't know why I'm here. I'm not good enough. I've only been dancing for a couple of years. Caitlyn keeps saying that only the best and brightest and most beautiful will be chosen. I should just go home now." A single tear rolled out of her left eye.

"You have just as much right to try out as she does. Maybe you won't get the lead, but there are a lot of smaller parts you'll be able to dance. Come on. We'll find Uncle Jeremy and you can warm up with us."

"Do you think it would be okay?" Marcie asked as she followed Remi from the restroom.

"He's a dancer, I'm a dancer, you're a dancer. Dancers dance, don't they?" Remi said. "Look, there's Uncle Jeremy now." Taking Marcie's hand, she dragged her down the hall.

"Ready Remi?" Jeremy straightened from where he'd been

leaning against the wall just out of sight of the lobby.

"This is Marcie. Can she warm up with us?" Remi pulled Marcie to stand before her uncle.

Jeremy looked the other girl up and down. She would be the perfect Sugar Plum Fairy. That was, if he were in charge of assigning roles. Remi, on the other hand with her natural gracefulness, would be perfect as Clara.

"Sure, come on. I didn't find a room, but there's plenty of hallway down here we can use," he said. He led the way down the hall and around the corner. "Okay ladies, let's get to work."

�〜

Remi followed her uncle, still dragging Marcie along with her, as if the other girl would disappear if she let go. She dropped her bag against the wall, then took up a position along the wall. There was a handrail that ran waist high down the length of the hall, which made a good barre. She heard Marcie move into position behind her as Jeremy began to count.

She bent and stretched, following his movements closely. These were stretches she did everyday, whether or not she danced, but doing the warm up with her uncle was different. She wanted to do them flawlessly and impress him, only he wasn't looking in her direction. Someday she wanted to be where he'd been, dancing on stages all around the world.

She heard whispers behind and around them but did not look around. Dancers dance. They concentrate and focus and don't let whispers in the background take their attention away from the slow count that directed them into deep pliés.

When Jeremy directed them to the floor, still not looking in their direction, Remi wondered what he was thinking about. The years of rehearsals and warm up just like this? The auditions he'd been to, either as a dancer or a judge? The fact that he was giving it all up?

"Concentrate, Remi," she whispered as she leaned over both legs, laying her chin on her knees and reaching past her toes to stretch the muscles up the back of her legs, her back, and all the way up her arms. She was so focused on the stretch that when soft music began to play, she didn't recognize it at first.

༄

Jeremy stretched as much as his knee would allow, focused on the job at hand. When the opening bars of *The Nutcracker*'s overture broke the silence, he looked over his shoulder. Besides Remi and Marcie there were eight other girls lined up down the hall behind him. He hadn't even heard them come in. Maybe they weren't the prettiest or the most popular, but these girls seemed willing to work hard. These were the kinds of dancers he'd dreamed of working with. An idea began to form in the back of his brain, unnoticed by the part that was busy stretching calf and lower back muscles.

He glanced at his watch and clapped his hands three times. "Ladies, it's two o'clock. Time to fly."

After his announcement, the girls politely chorused, "Thank you, Mr. Applewhite."

"You're very welcome," Jeremy said, remaining still while everyone around him scrambled to their feet.

He waited until everyone was out of sight before he struggled to stand. He bit his lip to stifle the groan that the pain of bending and movement brought forth. His muscles were warm and well stretched, but his left knee protested even that slight amount of work. How would he ever dance again if he couldn't even warm up properly?

As he walked to the lobby, he concentrated on not limping. He didn't want pity from these children. He wasn't sure what he did want, but it wasn't pity.

There were about twenty-five girls, still and silent, not like any group of teenage girls he'd ever been around. They should be bragging about the ballets that they'd danced in or talking about boys.

Circling around the girls, he headed toward a woman holding a notebook and a huge gym bag. She was a dancer, he decided. Tall yet lithe, she was like a willow that would gracefully bend and flow against a stiff breeze instead of breaking with a harsh crack.

Her features were irregular, her eyes too big and mouth too small for her heart-shaped face. Her nose seemed crooked, but it suited her, as did the wavy golden tresses she'd somehow managed to tame into a knot at the back of her head. Her gold-flecked violet eyes should clash with her hair, but somehow they complemented each other. Taken individually, her features were irregular, but together they created a unique face, instantly captivating him.

Then he listened to what she was saying.

"I'm sorry girls, but without a director and a choreographer, there's nothing I can do. The office is open for those of you who need to call for a ride."

"Hold on a minute, girls," Jeremy stepped in before the girls could react. "Wait right here for a couple of minutes. We might be able to work something out." Taking the beautiful dancer by the arm, he led her down the hall until they were out of earshot of the young crowd.

"What's going on?" he asked. He didn't let go of her until she pulled her arm from his grasp. Hers was a strong arm, slender, with long, well-toned muscles that were felt, but not seen. Her skin was the softest thing he'd ever felt.

"Who are you and why do you care?"

"My name is Jeremy Applewhite, and my niece is out there hoping to try out for your Christmas production. Why is it being canceled?"

The woman blinked twice and studied him closely before speaking. Recognition dawned, but then dimmed in her eyes. "Lynn Bowersox was the director and choreographer. Her husband called me this morning. She was in a car accident last night, and there's no way she'll be able to take charge."

"All you need is a director and choreographer? I'll do it," Jeremy volunteered without thinking twice.

"Mister, you don't know what's involved. There are a million headaches trying to put a production together. Especially when it's been advertised for the last three months as a new interpretation of an old classic."

"What's your name?" Jeremy didn't bother to argue with her. His mind was on the gold flecks in her eyes that almost overpowered the violet with their sparkle.

"Diane Cooper. I'm a dance instructor here in town. I was just supposed to help Lynn. I can't do it all by myself."

"I'll do it. But I've got to make a phone call before we start casting." Jeremy smiled at her. All at once he understood why he'd come home.

"Don't you want to know about the rehearsal schedule or your budget or anything?" Diane asked. She watched as he dug through his bag for his cell phone.

"We can talk about that later. Right now I need to make this call. Would you take the girls into the auditorium and line them up? Two rows with the girls an arm's length apart."

Jeremy dialed the number from memory, then turned away and leaned against the wall. He lifted his left leg. The knee was telling him that he'd reached his limit. He'd have to find a chair soon. As soon as he secured a surprise or two.

"Winston? It's Jeremy Applewhite."

❧

Winston Christopher sat up from where he'd been lying in bed, recuperating from a night that had lasted until after daybreak. He winced as the movement caused severe pain to several parts of his body. "Jeremy? Where are you? You missed the opening of the biggest flop on Broadway last night. Thank God, I didn't have anything to do with it."

Jeremy smiled. If it didn't have to do with theater, Winston wasn't interested. "You know that *Nutcracker* production you'd worked up for the children's ballet? The one they hated?"

"Yeah, what about it?"

"Is it still available?"

"You do mean the one the director told me shouldn't be performed even in Kansas?" Winston ran a hand through his hair and reached for the wire-rimmed glasses by the bed.

"Yeah, that one. I was wondering if you'd loan it to me. I'm working with a community group in Winchester, Virginia with no budget," Jeremy said.

"It is still available. I have all the notes and everything in a box here somewhere. I'll be happy to donate it," replied Winston.

"Can you send it to me ASAP? I need it yesterday. Everything you have. Music, costumes, notes, recordings, and set ideas you have as well. Harry has my address."

"Okay. I'll FedEx it to you," said Winston. "FedEx does deliver out there, doesn't it?"

"Yes, Winston. Thanks a bunch." Jeremy hung up, then hit speed dial for Harry's number.

After leaving instructions with Harry's voicemail, Jeremy

dropped the cell phone back into his bag. He headed toward the sound of chattering females, suddenly feeling like his life wasn't at an end after all.

At the doorway to the auditorium he paused, his gaze following Diane as she led the girls in warm ups. He limped to the middle of the auditorium. A table and several chairs faced the stage where the girls had taken their places. Dropping his bag, he slipped into a chair at one end of the table. He maneuvered another so he could rest his leg on it.

He pulled the abandoned clipboard closer and read over the notes already written there. The injured director had already decided on her cast. Picking up a pen, he made a giant X on the page, then flipped to a clean page. Looking over the girls, he started a list of rules for his dancers. Sweatshirts and pants, shorts and denim did not belong on stage. He didn't care about color, but the girls would wear leotards and tights with their dance shoes. Without Winston's choreography notes and music, there wasn't much he could do today except weed out the girls with two left feet or who had no rhythm.

Diane approached and knelt beside his chair. She didn't look very happy. She handed him a stack of papers. "Here are pictures and résumés from the girls that had them. The rest will bring them next time."

"Thanks. How many of these girls do you know?" Jeremy flipped through the stack. There was everything from blown up school pictures to professional portraits included. Remi was the only one who had an action picture. He paused at Marcie's, flipping it over and scanning the back. She was a beginner, but she would willingly throw herself in front of a train if he requested.

"I know about half of them. The others are from surrounding towns, and a couple of them are from West Virginia. I'm surprised we don't have a bigger turnout than this, really. How do you want to run the tryout?" Diane asked.

"I want to talk for a minute," Jeremy said. "Then we'll do some dancing. Do you have a routine you can teach them that will incorporate basic dance skills?"

"Ballet?"

"Not just ballet. The production we're going to do has some ballet, but also jazz, hiphop, soft-shoe. Anything you can throw at them. I want to see who can adapt to different dance styles." Jeremy replied.

"Yes, sir." Diane nodded, understanding his concept. She wasn't sure why world famous Jeremy Applewhite was here, but she'd let him lead the way—at least for now. If he screwed up, she'd step in and see if she could control the chaos. Judging from his accent and his expensive dance shoes, he was used to the best. He'd be the type to drive into D.C. when he needed to replace his jeans.

"Please, don't call me sir. Jeremy will be fine. After all, we'll be working closely together," *I hope*, he finished silently.

He pushed to his feet and swallowed the groan that rolled up. He slowly approached the stage, trying not to let his limp show.

"Good afternoon, ladies," he said.

"Good afternoon, Mr. Applewhite," the girls responded as they'd been taught in their very first dance lessons.

"As you've heard, Ms. Bowersox has been injured and will not be able to direct this year's production. If you'll allow me, I'd like to step in and take her place."

Immediately an excited murmur rose as the girls whispered amongst themselves. Jeremy allowed them a moment before clapping his hands three times. "I will be working you hard and will not allow for horseplay. Those of you who aren't willing to give one hundred ten percent can leave now. I have no use for you."

No one moved a muscle. After a moment, he continued.

"Ms. Cooper will be showing you some dance steps in a few minutes, and I want you to do them to the best of your ability. This will be the first round of auditions. Final auditions will be on Tuesday when I'll know exactly how many parts there are."

"Aren't we going to perform *The Nutcracker* like always?" Caitlyn asked from her front row position.

"Not this year. At least, not the same one you're used to. But more about that later. For now, I'll turn you over to Ms. Cooper."

৵

By the time Jeremy followed Diane out the door of the building, he'd fallen in love. But what to do about it when his future beyond Christmas was up in the air?

"I guess I'll see you Tuesday," she said. She locked the door and pocketed the key.

"Sure. 4:30, right?" Jeremy asked.

"Yes, 4:30. I'd better get going," Diane said. She shifted her bag from on shoulder to the other.

"You didn't drive?" Jeremy asked.

"No, I only live a couple of blocks from here."

"Remi and I would be glad to drop you off," he offered.

"That would be all right," Diane nodded in agreement.

Remi jumped into the back seat with a smile. Jeremy knew she'd be teasing him later about his obvious attraction to the dancing teacher.

Diane directed him to a three-story stone mansion in the historic district not far from the John Handley High School.

Until a few years before, the school had been a private boy's school, but progress had reached even Winchester, and now it was co-ed.

"You live here?" Remi asked, staring at the house, her eyes as big as plates.

"I live in an apartment on the third floor. There are four other apartments in the house." Diane turned to smile at the girl in the back seat.

"Does your husband live there with you?" Remi asked in the same awestruck tone.

"I'm not married," Diane responded with a telling glance in Jeremy's direction.

He raised his hands in surrender. "I don't have a thing to do with her nosiness," he said. "She gets that from her mother."

"Uh-huh," Diane said as she opened her door and slipped out. "Thanks for the ride. I'll see you Tuesday."

"Tuesday," Jeremy said. He sighed after she closed the door and walked up the stone walkway. He was mildly disappointed that she didn't glance back once.

Remi scrambled between the seats and took her place in the passenger's seat. "Uncle Jeremy's in love," she sang as she buckled her belt.

"Hush," Jeremy said, his face growing warm. He started the engine and pulled away from the curb, heading back to Romney.

"So what are we going to tell Mom and Dad? You're going to be spending a lot of time in Winchester getting everything together," Remi asked.

"We'll worry about that on Tuesday. I'd rather not lie to your parents. Maybe I'll tell them I got a job working for the Arts Council."

"But what about me? How am I going to get to go on Tuesday if I'm grounded?"

"We'll think of something." Jeremy said.

With that Remi nodded and laid her head back, falling asleep after only a few minutes. She didn't wake until Jeremy touched her shoulder.

"Remi, you're home," he said.

"Already? Wow, you drive fast!" Remi murmured between yawns.

"No, you were just tired."

Halfway to the house Remi stopped. "Uncle Jeremy, are you going to tell Mom and Dad about today?"

"Not yet. After we've both cemented our places with the company."

Remi thought it over, then nodded. "I guess that will be okay. But are you going to tell them about me?"

Jeremy paused for a moment. "I'm going to leave that bit of news up to you. Just remember I don't want to lie to your dad. There's been enough secrets without adding you into the mix."

"So, I have to tell them or else?" asked Remi.

Jeremy wrapped one arm around the girl. She looked much younger than her sixteen years. "Why don't we wait and see how things go on Tuesday. You may not have anything to tell them." He gave her an one-armed squeeze. "After all, you don't have a part, yet."

"But you have to give me a part, you're my uncle!" Remi said. She threw both arms around his waist and hugged him tight.

When she'd finished, he took a step back, then leaned over to look at her. "If you're going to dance professionally, you need to learn something right now. Nothing in life is guaranteed. My being your uncle will have nothing to do with your winning a role. You will earn your part just like all the others. Talent lands roles, not who you know. Understand what I'm saying?"

"Yeah, I think so. Hard work counts more than having an uncle who's the director of the production," Remi said.

"Smart girl," Jeremy said. He ruffled her hair in a way he hoped was still allowed.

"Hey, you two coming in for dinner or what?" Stacy called from the front porch.

"Yes, ma'am," Jeremy said. He nudged Remi with his shoulder, then followed her across the yard. All at once he was starving.

14

Just after dawn Tuesday morning, the doorbell rang three times in rapid succession. Jeremy rolled over and frowned in concentration. There had been no bells in his dream. The phone beside the bed wasn't ringing. What was it? Then the bell sounded again. Was that the front doorbell? No one ever came to the front door. Everyone came to the back porch and banged on the screen door a couple of times before letting themselves in. Even the FedEx man who delivered two packages just the day before knew to come to the back door.

"Must be some lost-out-of-town fool," Jeremy muttered. He threw back the covers and pulled on a pair of light cotton pants. Then he climbed from the bed and headed to the door. Using furniture for balance, he heavily favored his bad leg. As he threw open the door, he growled, "What the hell do you want?"

"Well, that's a hell of a way to greet your savior. Thank God you're not toting a shotgun!" The man stepped back down two steps.

"Winston? What the hell are you doing here? Has the New York theater crowd finally come to its senses and thrown you out of the state?" Jeremy wiped one hand over his face and looked again. First he took in the man on the stoop, then the number of bag and boxes lined up across the front yard. He'd come to stay awhile.

In deference to comfort, Winston was dressed in a deep plum sweat suit with a lemon yellow T-shirt. The shirt matched his sun-bright yellow sneakers.

Thankfully, he hadn't dyed his dirty-blonde hair to match. It might be thinner on top than the last time Jeremy had seen him, but still caught at the nape of his neck in a clip before trailing in ringlets halfway to his waist. The mustache was new, probably a camouflage for the fact that Winston had no noticeable upper lip.

The pile of luggage was a warning. Winston had not come for just a day or two. "I didn't find the box until it was too late to ship it, so I decided to deliver it in person. That way I can see how the rural set lives and answer the question on everyone's lips about you, my dear boy." Winston embraced Jeremy for just a second before turning to his belongings. "Be a dear and help me with my things."

"Leave them for now. I need coffee." Jeremy said. He pushed open the screen door for his guest, then turned and headed for the kitchen.

"So the rumors floating about town are true. You've been injured." Winston said. He left the door open so he could keep an eye on the front yard. He wasn't quite as certain as his friend that his things were safe if left unattended.

Ten minutes later, the two men sat at the kitchen table with coffee. "How long are you going to stay?" Jeremy asked. From the looks of the pile on the front lawn, Winston would be staying through spring.

"It depends on how long it takes you to catch on and see my vision. What's with the gimpy leg?" Winston asked. He nodded to where Jeremy had propped his leg on a chair. "The truth, my friend. Did it go during your last performance? That's the story that everyone's telling everyone else."

"That last leap across the stage didn't help the seventeen years of damage already done. Truth is I was trying to keep up with my brother and landed wrong. I'm off stage for a while. Maybe permanently."

"Great! Now you can take charge of the new company I'm putting together. A company like no other," Winston gushed. He set his mug down with a thump and clapped like a child. "With your experience and name and my vision and name, we could set the dance world on its collective ears!"

"Winston, remember the reason you're here? I've got a gig that lasts through Christmas. Then I'm to have surgery and rehabilitation. If I'm still not able to return to the stage, then and only then will I talk to you about working together. Understand?"

"Completely. You're terrified," Winston said. He'd had never known Jeremy to not talk about the future before. Usually he planned a year ahead. For now, they'd take it one week at a time and revisit the idea of a partnership in the spring.

"I'm not terrified. Well, not much. I've been a dancer my whole life. I don't know what I'll do if I…"

"If you can't dance anymore?"

"Yeah," Jeremy said. He swallowed hard, trying to keep his panic at bay. Winston surprised him by being able to see his fear. "For now I want to concentrate on this production."

"Great! Let's bring in my things and, after I unpack, we can look at what I brought."

⌇

"Hey Jeremy, you okay? Mrs. Allbright called and told me to get over here. She wanted to make sure you weren't dead or anything," Chance called. He pushed open the door and walked into the house.

He'd been about to leave for the restaurant when the phone had rung. Reverend Allbright's wife had carried on about a wild looking stranger carrying boxes and bags into Dottie's house. She didn't like the look of the stranger and thought Chance ought to make sure everything was okay.

Jeremy wasn't in the kitchen, but the stranger Mrs. Allbright had called about was. Papers were scattered over every flat surface in the room. Table, counters, and stove were covered. They were even stuck to the refrigerator with magnets.

Winston looked up from where he was studying a sheaf of papers. "Hello. Jeremy's busy right now."

Chance cocked his head as he studied the stranger. "Who the hell are you?"

"Winston Christopher, choreographer extraordinaire. You must be Jeremy's brother. Welcome to Chaos Central." Winston returned his attention to the papers in his hand. Finally, he tossed them in the air. They spread across the floor and he knelt to pick them up one by one, putting them in order as he did.

Chance didn't know what to make of the stranger, so he headed for the living room. Jeremy was lying on the couch wearing headphones. One eye was closed as the other scanned the open notebook before him. He was so lost in what he was doing that he didn't notice Chance cross the room. It wasn't until Chance switched off the tape player that Jeremy returned from the faraway world he'd been visiting.

The musical interpretation Winston had come up with was incredible. With had work from the girls and a few lucky breaks, he might, just might, be able to put Winston's production on stage in two months.

"Chance? What are you doing here?" Jeremy sat up and arched his back, feeling four vertebrae shift back into more comfortable positions.

"Who the hell is in the kitchen?" Chance lowered his voice to an intense whisper, though he knew any sound carried through the house like a shout.

"Winston Christopher. Didn't he introduce himself?" Jeremy remained vague. His thoughts were still visualizing the dance Winston had choreographed, and making necessary changes.

"So what is Winston Christopher doing here?" Chance wanted to either shake his brother or pour cold water on him. Something to focus his brain on the here and now. He'd always been this way, focused to the exclusion of everything else, even eating or sleeping. Obviously that intensity hadn't changed in the time he'd been away.

"He's helping me with a project," Jeremy answered, his voice foggy with distraction. "Hey Winston, we need to cut the cast down to fifteen, and even that will be stretching the talent pool."

Winston appeared in the doorway and leaned against it. "How about cutting out the largest group dances? Or maybe tapping the local theater group to help out? Surely there are fifty dancers around here somewhere."

"I doubt it. You'll understand better when you see the stage," Jeremy replied. "I have a couple of ideas I want to run by you. We've got to make it as easy as possible. We're talking about a group of young women who love to dance."

"They'll be professional by the time we're through with them," Winston predicted before returning to the kitchen. "I'm fixing lunch, do you want something?"

"Yeah, whatever," Jeremy answered. His mind returned to the notebook and he began scribbling.

Chance was amazed at the ease with which these two worked together. Obviously, they'd collaborated before. Grabbing Jeremy's notebook with both hands, he yanked it out of his brother's grip before taking a step backward.

"Hey, give that back!" Jeremy pushed to his feet, lunging toward his brother, and almost fell on his face when his knee gave way.

"I need your attention. We have a meeting at the bank at one-thirty with Dottie's attorney. Wear something casual, but not your dance clothes." Chance closed the notebook and held it behind his back.

"Why?"

"For the reading of the will."

"Okay, but I have to be out of there by three o'clock. I'll pick Remi up from school and take her with me this afternoon," Jeremy said. He held out his hand for the notebook. "And don't count on us being back for dinner."

"Don't keep her out too late. She has school in the morning." Chance ordered. He returned the notebook, then pulled an envelope out of his back pocket. "You might want to look this over before the meeting." He handed it to his brother and turned to leave.

In the kitchen, Winston had filled two plates with leftovers, making them as attractive as something served in a four-star restaurant. He glanced at Chance then reached for another plate. "Will you be joining us?"

"No thanks, I have to get to work," Chance said. He was bewildered by this man his brother called friend.

"Well, then it was nice meeting you," Winston said. He wiped his hand on the towel he'd tucked into the waistband of his pants, then extended it.

"Yeah, nice," Chance said as he shook the other man's hand. "Make sure he gets to the bank by one-thirty, okay?"

"Certainly. Jeremy always gets lost in a new production. That's why I decided to come for a visit. Someone has to take care of our boy," Winston said.

"Yeah, right." Chance took his hand back and left. He'd have to ask some tactfully probing questions of his brother, but later when they were alone.

As he crossed the yard he heard Winston call, "Jeremy, come eat your lunch. Have you taken your medicine yet?"

⤳

The large clock on the wall showed 1:27 when Jeremy entered the lobby of the First National Bank of Romney. Of course, Chance was already there, waiting in a chair next to the receptionist's desk. Jeremy took the seat beside him.

"Did Dottie really leave anything?" Jeremy asked.

"We'll know in a few minutes." Chance nodded toward the attorney who'd just breezed into the building.

Jeremy turned and froze. He recognized that body. The navy suit skimmed her body, hinting at the curves her leotard had vividly outlined. She was a dancer, not an attorney.

A moment later, Diane Cooper met his gaze squarely. She lifted her chin a notch. Was she challenging him to comment on her two disparate sides?

"Diane, thanks for coming over for this. We really appreciate it," Chance said. He crossed the lobby floor, hand outstretched in welcome.

"You know I'd do anything for Dottie. She was a special lady," Diane said. She returned his handshake before turning in Jeremy's direction. "Hello, Jeremy. Good to see you again." She sounded ultra-professional as she held out her hand.

Jeremy swallowed hard, then cleared his throat. Diane Cooper in a dance leotard was one thing. In the navy-blue power suit, she was spectacular. "I'm surprised to see you here," he said softly.

Jeremy lost himself in her eyes. He wanted to sweep her off her feet, carry her to his car, and take her back to Dottie's house. The only problem was that he could barely keep himself upright. Plus there was Winston to think about. No matter how tempting, he couldn't kick his friend out only hours after his arrival.

Jeremy was so lost in daydreams that he almost didn't hear Chance say, "Diane has been Dottie's attorney since Leland White retired five years ago. Last spring, she had the nerve to move to Winchester."

"It's not like I left town never to return. I still have office hours here twice a week," Diane argued with a smile.

"It's not the same as having you around full time," Chance said. "I miss you in dance class."

"Miss Cooper? Mr. Kendall is ready for you in the conference room," the receptionist broke in.

"Mr. Kendall?" Jeremy asked as he and Chance followed the two women across the lobby. Jeremy trailed Diane, breathing deeply of the delicate apple scent that drifted his way. She reminded him of the fall he'd picked apples for extra money for new dance shoes.

"He's the bank president," Chance explained.

Jeremy nodded as they entered the conference room. After formal introductions and condolences, the four settled at the table, Chance and Jeremy on one side and the professionals on the other.

"If it's all right with you gentleman, I'll dispense with the formalities and cut to the meat of the will," Diane said. She pulled a file from her briefcase and opened it in front of her.

"Sure, go ahead," Chance approved after Jeremy nodded in agreement.

"Okay, the gist of the will is that you will divide things equally, except..."

"Except?" questioned Chance.

"Except for the separate money market accounts she set up with the money you were giving her each month. The house she left to you both, but if neither of you want it, she asked that you consider donating it to the county Women's Shelter." Diane read from her notes. "The contents of the house and everything else is to be divided between you."

"She didn't use the money we sent?" Jeremy asked.

"She had a well-financed retirement fund and she lived frugally. She said she didn't want to hurt your feelings, so she invested it for your futures," Diane said as she blinked back her tears.

"Where did she get the money to loan me for the restaurant?" Chance asked, stunned by this revelation.

"She told me the money came from Jeremy and that as you paid her back, she returned the money to his account."

"That wily old skinflint," Jeremy chuckled as he shook his head.

"Well, brother, thanks for the help. One of these nights you'll have to come by and have dinner," Chance said.

"If you gentleman will sign this paperwork, we'll transfer the accounts into your names. Unless you're planning to close these accounts?" Mr. Kendall asked, clearly bothered by the possibility.

Jeremy tried to remember how much money he'd sent

Dottie over the years, but he was a dancer, not a banker. He looked to Diane and asked, "How much money are we talking about?"

Instead of answering, the bank president handed him a folder. "This will explain your account and its contents."

Jeremy accepted the file with his name on it, then opened it. He fought to keep from gasping. Dottie had done well with the money he'd sent her, more than doubling the amount to a nest egg that would more than keep him going for quite a while, while he decided his future. Chance gasped beside him, pale as he turned to meet his own shocked gaze.

"If you'll read the papers, then sign at the bottom of page one and initial the two highlighted lines on page two, we'll set up your accounts."

"Mr. Kendall, I have an appointment I must leave for now. I'd like to come back tomorrow and take care of this, as well as set up a checking account."

"Certainly, certainly. I'll hold onto those papers until then," Mr. Kendall said as he accepted the file back with a relieved smile.

"Now if you'll excuse me, I have to pick up Remi," Jeremy said, pushing to his feet slowly.

"If you have any further questions, call me," Diane said. She stood as well, tossing files back into her briefcase.

"Uh, sure. Don't forget Jeremy, my daughter has school tomorrow. Don't keep her out all night."

"I'll have Winston watch the clock for me. We'll get her home before ten," Jeremy said.

Jeremy left the conference room, crossed the lobby, and didn't stop until he was outside the bank. He waited there until Diane stopped beside him.

"Winston?" She asked, raising one eyebrow in his direction.

"Winston Christopher, our choreographer. I have to pick him up, then Remi," Jeremy fought the urge to lean down and kiss her.

"Sure. See you there," Diane said.

Jeremy watched her climb into her hunter green GMC Jimmy, entranced by her graceful movements. "You've got it bad, boy. Get your mind out of the gutter. You can't spend the evening ogling your assistant," Jeremy muttered to himself as he climbed into his car.

Hopefully, Winston had made some order out of the box of loose papers he'd arrived with. With the production tape playing on the car stereo, Jeremy shifted his thoughts from family to work.

15

$\mathcal{R}$emi wished there was some exercise or magic potion that would make her nerves settle down. She wanted to pace or practice her audition routine one last time, but that wasn't allowed. She had to sit quietly with the others who were waiting their turns to go onstage and impress Jeremy and his two assistants.

Instead of picking and choosing or lining the girls alphabetically, they all warmed up together, then Diane handed each girl a piece of paper with two identical numbers on it. The girls had to tear the paper in half and put one number in the bright purple cowboy hat that Diane passed around. Then the girls moved offstage and waited.

Jeremy reached into the hat, pulled out a number, and then called it out so the girls were dancing in absolute random order. So far twelve girls had danced. There were ten left when Jeremy called, "Number twenty to the stage please."

Remi looked at her paper, double-checking that her number hadn't changed. No, she was still number twenty. She rose and walked to the stage steps. It was hard not to race onto the stage, throw herself on her knees in front of her uncle and beg to be released from this torture. But that wasn't how auditions worked.

Remi handed Diane her slip of paper and the CD she'd brought with her. "Track three, please," she whispered. Then she took her place in the middle of the stage.

She closed her eyes, took a deep breath, and listened for the music. Then she began to dance. The fluttering nerves and queasy stomach disappeared as the music took over her body. She floated, leapt, and twirled across the stage, each movement her own and practiced time and time again. When she finished the part that she knew by heart, she planned to stop. But the music held her enthralled and refused to release her from its spell. She continued dancing until the last chord played, moving with grace and beauty through unrehearsed steps. She ended up curled in a ball, out of breath and wishing someone had videotaped the last three minutes of her life. She'd never remember the unchoreographed moves she'd just performed otherwise.

Taking one last deep breath, she rose to her feet and turned to the table at the side of the stage. The three adults looked stunned. "Thank you," Remi said with a nod before turning and leaving the stage.

It was over and she'd survived. She hadn't thrown up, fallen off the stage, or tripped over her own feet. By the time she settled back in her seat, she was grinning with happiness. She'd done it, and from the whispers of those around her, she had performed well. Pulling out a small notebook from her bag, she tried to recreate on paper the steps that she'd just performed. She didn't watch the rest of the auditions. She survived hers and for now, that was all she cared about.

It was over an hour later after the last girl danced.

"Okay, ladies, that's it for today. We'll announce roles next time. Mr. Christopher and I will share the story with you then as well," Jeremy said.

They'd found a fairly comfortable leather wingback chair in the prop room and moved it to the middle of the auditorium. After leading the girls through their warm ups, he had collapsed into the chair. His knee throbbed, reminding him that he'd left his pain pills at home.

Home. How quickly he'd come to think of Dottie's wooden frame house as home again. If he stayed in Romney, he would make a few changes, but so far he was happy, even if he didn't know where his life was heading.

"Take this," Winston said. He shoved a hand in front of Jeremy's nose. There was a single white tablet in the center of his palm.

"Bless you, my friend," he said. By the time they were ready to head back over the mountain, the pill would have taken the edge off. Maybe he'd be able to concentrate on something other than throbbing ache.

He watched the girls leave the room. Only Remi and Marcie remained behind. They went onto the stage and stood facing each other at center stage. Then Remi taught the other girl her special dance. Marcie wasn't as experienced, but after watching the audition piece once again, when Remi started over, she was moving in mirror image to her new friend. Her adaptability would serve her well in the weeks to come. Jeremy would be throwing new sequences at the girls on an almost daily basis.

"She's a good teacher," Diane said, reentering the room. The other girls had been delivered to their waiting mothers, who'd been banned from the auditorium during rehearsals. Jeremy refused to deal with parents. The only way to avoid the hassles they presented was to outlaw them from seeing the production until the last possible moment.

"Just like her mother. She also has an excellent student. Marcie would be a good prince since we have an absence of male performers," Jeremy said.

"And Clara? Please, not Caitlyn," Winston pleaded, his

notebook opened to his list of the girls and their strengths and weaknesses. "She has no depth and so much conceit she makes even you appear humble."

Jeremy chuckled. He had never been the most humble of dancers simply because he was the best. If you're the best and know it, why be humble? You don't get work by downplaying your abilities.

Caitlyn, though she could dance ballet, didn't have the depth they were looking for in the lead. This was not your typical production of *The Nutcracker*. The lead would need to be versatile as well as good.

"If we go with Remi it might look like favoritism." Jeremy approached the subject cautiously.

"No, it won't. I overheard the other girls murmuring about how good she is. She's also got the range you wanted. She'd be perfect for the role, no matter what you ask of her," Diane said. It was time to make her feelings known though she still didn't know what the production would call for.

"Sorry Monsieur Director, but you've been outvoted. Remi will be Clara and Marcie, the prince. The problem will be Uncle and the other adult parts," Winston said, brushing flyaway strands of hair out of his eyes.

"I have a couple of adults in my classes who said they'd be happy to help as long as they didn't have large parts. They dance for the exercise, not for the stage," Diane offered. "I also know a man who could dance the part of Uncle. I talked to his wife today, and she said they'd both be happy to help."

"Contact them and have them come to Thursday's rehearsal so everyone will hear the same version of the story," Jeremy said. The girls onstage had given up on Remi's audition piece and were bopping to the music from the boombox's radio.

They looked good together and would make a good match. Since this was a production of youngsters, he wouldn't demand lifts or mile high jumps, unless Remi felt so inclined. Having her as Clara allowed him to work with her on the days they didn't have rehearsals. Maybe Marcie would be able to join them in Romney for some rehearsal time as well.

"Remi, let's go. Your dad's going to skin me alive if I don't get you home so you can do your homework." Jeremy bent his knee carefully and pushed himself out of the chair, careful to suppress the groan of protest.

"Can we give Marcie a ride home? She lives in Augusta and her mom can't come and get her," Remi asked. The girls pulled on sweats over their dance clothes, then sat down and traded their dance shoes for sneakers.

"Sure. Does she go to school with you?" Jeremy asked.

"Yeah, but she's a grade ahead of me."

Jeremy filed the information away for future reference. He also saw Winston scribbling furiously in his book. Obviously, his friend was reading his mind again.

"All right, ladies. Take this stuff out to the car and we'll head home."

Diane remained silent, watching the man she idolized limp across the auditorium. She knew from talking with Winston that his career was over. This opportunity to direct was a test. Did he have what it took to be in charge? Better to find out now in a very small, local production than on a national stage.

By watching him interact with the girls, she knew he would do just fine. He wouldn't stay in the mountains for long. He was a world famous performer. Once he'd completed his knee surgery and therapy, he would be in demand as a director or the head of a dance company or maybe a judge on one of those television reality dance shows. She'd still be here dancing and teaching each evening as a way to make ends meet. No one wanted to take a chance on a young female attorney whose roots weren't planted in the mountains five generations ago.

"Diane, are you ready?" Jeremy asked.

Diane blinked and nodded. "Yes, I'm ready. Let me just tell Mrs. Kelly that the karate class can have the room."

She hurried away, needing to get out of Jeremy Applewhite's hypnotic realm. If she stayed around him much longer, she would blurt out her secret. And that was the last thing either of them needed. He did not need to know that she'd been infatuated with him since the first time she'd seen him onstage almost twelve years ago. She had to see him as more than dark hair, flashing eyes, and a body that interpreted music like no one else.

"Miss Cooper, are you finished? We do have others waiting to use that room," Mrs. Kelly said. She was the center's scheduling secretary, a watchdog of a woman who was built like a bulldog.

"I'm sorry, Mrs. Kelly, but we have a new director," Diane said.

"We cannot have you running twenty minutes over every time. The karate class is supposed to have that room at seven o'clock, not seven-twenty. Please make sure to pass that along to your new director."

"I'll do that. Have a nice evening." Diane shifted her bag and headed out. The karate class had moved into the auditorium. The dancers were gone. Even Jeremy and his entourage had left.

Jeremy Applewhite. She shook her head as she pushed open the door and stepped onto the sidewalk. She shouldn't be thinking about the man. She shouldn't be thinking about any man. She should be concentrating on work. She still had several precedents to look up before her meeting in the morning.

"Having second thoughts?" Jeremy asked softly, appearing at her left elbow from the shadows near the doorway.

"Oh! I thought you'd left," Diane said.

"Not yet. I sent Winston and Remi for dinner. I wanted to talk to you alone for a minute," Jeremy said. He stepped closer, the need to touch this beautiful woman overruling good sense. They were standing in a public parking lot with people coming and going, but they only had eyes for each other.

"What about?" Diane took a half step, drawn toward this man like metal filings to a magnet.

"Second thoughts about working on this production. Are you regretting your choice?" Jeremy asked.

"Of course not. Why would I?"

"Because I've never directed before and my choreographer is about as organized as a tornado." Jeremy used two fingers to smooth a loose strand of hair back from her face. "You are so damn beautiful," he murmured before closing the distance between them. In front of God and anyone else who cared to look, Jeremy Applewhite kissed Diane Cooper.

He brushed his lips across hers once, then again. Shifting closer, he deepened the kiss. Every thought she'd had about this man, any thought she'd had about any man fled as she parted her lips. Shifting his head farther to the right, Jeremy released her for a second as he prepared for some serious mindless kissing.

"Dinner's getting cold, Uncle Jeremy," the young female voice broke through the fog that had encapsulated her brain. It brought her back to Earth with a not quite audible crash.

It took a moment for them to comprehend that someone

was pulling on his elbow, trying to get his attention. He pulled back, breaking the kiss. He didn't release her, didn't move more than a few inches. Her hands rested at his waist, not fighting, but not pulling him back, either.

"Come on, the chicken's getting cold!" The voice intruded again.

Diane blinked, shocked at what they'd done and where they'd done it.

"Join us for dinner?" Jeremy whispered.

"All right," Diane agreed as she leaned back.

Now there was an inch of space between their bodies as well as their lips. If she were stronger, she'd step back and slap the man. But he'd only done what her heart had begged him to do.

Grabbing Jeremy, Remi pulled on his arm. "Come on, let's eat. I'm starving!"

Jeremy took a step to accommodate her pull. His gaze never left Diane's. Taking her hand, he pulled Diane after them. "Come on, let's eat. She's starving."

Diane blinked, then giggled. She'd always expected to fall for another attorney or an accountant, someone with a similar background and future. Never would she have dreamed she would fall for the most famous dancer to come out of West Virginia.

"I like that sound," Jeremy said a bright smile.

Diane blushed, not sure how to respond. Should she act like the kiss never happened? Or beg for another to confirm the magic between them?

16

"Do you ever have regrets?" Stacy asked over take-out boxes of spaghetti and meatballs. They sat in the middle of the studio floor eating between classes. In a few minutes, Chance would take over and teach the evening class so she could go home.

"Regrets about what?" Chance asked. He looked up, baffled by the question. Stacy had been in a pensive mood ever since his arrival twenty minutes before.

"About not following Jeremy out into the dance world. About not being a dancer instead of a dance teacher. You gave up your life's dream for a wife and a child." Stacy studied the man next to her through tear-filled eyes.

Chance froze, stunned by her question. Obviously, these thoughts had been troubling her for quite awhile. "Of course I've had regrets, but not about you or Remi or our life together. I sometimes wish I could have danced professionally, but dreams change. I have a wonderful family and the restaurant and this place where I share what I love with others." Chance set his dinner down. He pulled Stacy into his arms. "I'm very happy with my life and don't want to be anywhere but where I am right now. Okay?"

Stacy nodded. "Would you dance onstage now if you were given the chance?"

"I'm too old for the life of a dancer, honey," Chance said as he wiped her face dry. He kissed her cheek and picked up his dinner again.

"But if you could, would you?"

"If somebody wanted this old man in their production, I guess I could cooperate."

"Good. I have a job for you," Stacy said with a sexy smile. "They need a male dancer for their Christmas production. I told her you'd do anything you could to help."

"They who? She who? What, exactly, have you volunteered me for, Wife?"

"While Diane was in town today, she asked if you would be interested in dancing in their production of *The Nutcracker* this year. I told her we'd both be happy to help in any way we can." Stacy dropped her chin and smiled, her eyes glinting through her eyelashes. "You will help, won't you? They're raising money for the children's library this year. You're the only male dancer in fifty miles who is talented enough to be of any real help." Leaning toward him, Stacy brushed a string of kisses along his jaw line.

Chance purred deeply before saying, "You know I'll do anything for you. Who's in charge this year?"

"Lynn Bowersox was supposed to be, but she's broken her leg. Diane said the new director is sure to garner a lot of attention and raise a pile of money, but wouldn't say anything more than that."

"As long as I don't have to direct, I guess I've been volunteered," Chance said. He kissed his wife on the cheek before turning back to his dinner.

"Thanks, sweetheart."

"No more worrying about regrets, okay? Otherwise I'll take you into that closet you call an office and keep you there until I've proven that I am very happy with my life."

"Eat your dinner, Romeo. Your ladies will be here in few minutes," Stacy ordered in her loving way.

~

After dinner, Winston dropped Diane off at her apartment. Then he made his way to Highway 50 and turned toward Romney. The only sound were whispers and occasional giggles from the back seat. When they reached Augusta, Marcie pointed out her house. The two and a half story farmhouse sat on the right side of the highway. The driveway wound behind the house. Winston followed the drive and stopped at the back door.

"Thanks for the ride. See you tomorrow, Remi," Marcie said politely before she climbed out of the back seat.

"See you Thursday at rehearsal," Jeremy said.

"Yes, sir. I'll be there." She closed the door and rounded the car. Her mother waited in the doorway.

The rest of the ride was silent. When Jeremy began to snore, Remi leaned forward between the seats to give Winston directions. When they reached her house, she leaned forward to kiss her uncle's cheek before climbing out of the back seat.

"See you Thursday, Winston," she called over her shoulder.

"I look forward to it, my dear," Winston said with a thoughtful smile. She would be the perfect Clara. He began humming "Clara's Theme" as he waited for her to go inside. Only after the door was closed did he put the car in gear.

Jeremy waited until Winston was driving away before groaning, "She's only sixteen years old."

"She dances like a dream. For a child growing up in the back of beyond, she's surprisingly well read and has a maturity beyond her years," Winston pointed out gently.

"She's still only sixteen years old," Jeremy responded.

He stretched from his hips to his shoulders. The few minutes of sleep he'd managed did little to dispel his exhaustion. He'd started yawning during their impromptu picnic across the street from the Arts Center. All he wanted was to sprawl across Dottie's queen-size bed and sleep for a dozen hours.

By the time they cruised into town, Jeremy was dozing. He didn't feel the turn into the driveway or the engine die. Bright light woke him as Winston opened his door. They were home. He couldn't remember much after dropping Remi off. Lord, he was tired.

Taking a deep breath, he opened the door with one hand while punching the seatbelt release with the other. He didn't try to stifle a groan as he pushed himself from the front seat. He lurched across the lawn to the back porch, his crutches the only thing keeping him on his feet.

Winston followed, carrying his duffle bag and the box that held the papers he had managed to make sense of. He had two days to organize his notes and share his vision with Jeremy. Once inside, Jeremy continued to his room. Winston stopped in the kitchen long enough to drop his load. He poured a glass of milk and carried it to Jeremy's bedroom.

Stepping through the doorway, Winston flipped on the light. Surprisingly, Jeremy had already stripped and was under the covers. He opened his eyes to half-mast when Winston held the milk out.

"Drink this," he ordered.

"Go away. I don't need it. I need twelve hours of sleep," Jeremy grumbled. He rolled over, showing Winston the broad expanse of tanned back above the edge of the sheet and blankets.

"I'm not leaving until you drink your milk. Shall I recite poetry or sing for your entertainment while I wait?"

Jeremy sat up and glared at the smaller man. "Don't sing. Anything but singing."

"For my first selection, I'll begin with 'Danny Boy'," Winston said with a smirk. He couldn't carry a tune unless it was in a bucket, but that didn't stop him from torturing poor souls like Jeremy once in a while.

"Give me the glass," Jeremy relented. He chugged the cold milk like it was a beer. He didn't take a breath until he handed the glass back to his friend. "Now go away. I'm exhausted."

"Certainly. Sleep well," Winston said. He turned off the light as he left the room.

After he straightened the kitchen and living room, he retreated to his bedroom on the second floor. If he spent any more time downstairs, he'd be scrubbing the bathtub and singing to himself, which would surely wake Jeremy. Once in his room, he kicked off his shoes and tried to relax. He tried to read the latest thriller everyone was talking about. He tried to write a letter to Mitchell, who was currently directing a musical in London. He tried to decide which of the adult roles in the production he could perform. Not because he could dance, but he could be another warm body to fill in the background. No matter what he did, he couldn't settle his mind down. It would be hours before he could sleep. If he stayed here, he'd only disturb Jeremy, who needed his sleep.

"Time to find the pubs in town," he murmured, slipping his shoes back on.

He pulled on a light jacket and headed into town on foot. No need to take the car. He'd rambled miles in the city; here it was only a few blocks to the only place that was open. "The Brass Rail, sports bar, grill, and restaurant," he read. "Hope they serve more than beer, nachos, and spicy wings."

꒰ꜛ꒱

Jeremy woke humming the closing song of Winston's production. He felt better than he had in weeks. Even his knee
was giving him a break. He'd seen the production. His dreams
had shown him the costumes, dances, sets, and which girl
would fit into each role.

Grabbing the legal pad and ballpoint pen from the bed-
side table, he began scribbling notes as fast as his hand could
move. He had to record the impressions before they slipped
away like the first frost under the early morning sun.

"I do believe you've got it, old man," he murmured as he
finished the cast list. "Now all you have to do is build the sets,
make the costumes, and teach the girls their parts."

Climbing out of bed, he showered, then pulled on
yesterday's sweatpants. Limping to the kitchen he sniffed
the air, but didn't smell coffee. Winston always had coffee
ready by the time he crawled out, but this morning, the
coffeemaker was empty.

Jeremy loaded water and coffee into the machine, then
flipped it on. He slowly climbed the stairs. "Hey Winston,
haul it on out! We have a ton of work to do." He pushed
open the bedroom door with a crutch and peered inside.

Winston wasn't in the bed. He wasn't in the room. Except for the open briefcase on the bed, it looked as if he hadn't
been home. His notebook was missing.

Movement on the lawn caught his attention. Moving to
the window, he watched the sheriff's SUV pull in next to
Winston's Mercedes. The sheriff climbed from the driver's
side and rounded the front of the truck.

"Holy Hannah!" Jeremy swore softly when the sheriff
opened the passenger's door and helped Winston from the
front seat.

As fast as his bad knee would allow, Jeremy descended the stairs. Just as he entered the kitchen, a thump, thump, thump boomed through the house. Opening the door, Jeremy's stunned gaze bounced from his friend to the sheriff and back again.

Winston looked grim, bloody, and not like himself. His ponytail was missing. His face was black and blue and purple along the left side. His lip was bleeding. One shirtsleeve was torn from his shirt. The arm not clutching his notebook and jacket to his chest was protecting his side.

"You know this man, Jeremy?" The sheriff had been portly when Jeremy was in high school. Now he was a walking house. He still wore the gold badge that read Sheriff of Hampshire County on his starched white dress shirt.

"Yes, sir. He's a friend from New York," Jeremy said. He stepped aside when Winston stumbled toward him, mayhem in his expression. Jeremy let him pass, then turned back to the sheriff. "What happened?"

"Emmett Johnson and his boys were in town celebrating Milo's release from jail. They got a little out of hand. Your friend made some comment or another and the boys used him as a punching bag. They claimed to be giving him a haircut, but I think they were trying to beat the fag out of him. I took him to the jail for the night to keep him out of trouble."

"Thanks, sheriff," Jeremy shook the man's hand, then closed the door when the other man turned and left.

Turning to his friend, he swore. "What the hell happened?" He limped to the coffeemaker and poured two cups of coffee.

"I'd rather not talk about it just now," Winston grumbled. He sipped at his coffee, grimacing when the hot liquid burned the cut in his lip. He didn't say another word as he drank the coffee one or two sips at a time. When he finished, he set down the mug and pushed out of his chair. His expression was one of pained concentration. "I'm going to get cleaned up."

"When you're done I want to tell you what I came up with," Jeremy replied. He hoped talking of the production would take his friend's mind off his embarrassment and pain.

17

"Who was that?" Chance asked as Stacy rolled out of bed.

"Jeremy. Seems his friend had some trouble with the Johnson boys last night. He needs some first aid and Jeremy asked if I could stop by. Something about bruises, banged up egos, and bad haircuts." Stacy said. She pulled on panties and a sports bra, then a sweatshirt and jeans.

She shoved her feet into sneakers as she scraped her hair back. She anchored the ponytail with a purple scrunchie that clashed with her sweatshirt. But she didn't care. She hadn't met Winston yet and was looking forward to meeting the internationally famous choreographer. Maybe he could work up a little something for her girls to do for their Christmas pageant.

"You sure can dress quick when you want to. How fast can you strip?" Chance asked. He sat up in the bed and stretched.

He wasn't sure he liked the way his wife leapt at Jeremy's call. But what could he do? If he told her not to go he'd sound jealous. If he didn't react, it would seem like he didn't care. He did care, more than he'd admit to anyone, himself included.

Leaning over the bed, she gave him a quick kiss. She didn't linger long. If she did, he'd have her back to bare skin in no time. "You have mornings this week, remember?" she said as his alarm began chirping.

"Yeah," Chance he rolled out and padded to the bathroom. "I'll see you later."

But she was already gone. As she descended the stairs, she tried to remember if her first aid kit was in her car or in the pantry where she kept it when not on call. Stopping in front of Remi's closed door, she knocked three times, paused for a second then opened the door. "Good morning sunshine. Time to rise and shine."

"Mmmrrph," was the only response from the lump laying cattycorner across the mattress.

"Roll out. You're dad will be down in a few minutes. You want him to wake you up?"

The covers moved and a head emerged. "No way! The last time he used frozen marbles!"

"So get up and save him from having to find the marbles." Stacy grinned. The marbles were hidden behind the flour in the pantry. One place Chance would never look.

"Okay. I'm up. Thanks, Mom." Remi wasn't awake enough to ask where her mother was off to so early in the day. Probably one of the neighbors had an emergency only her mom could deal with. They'd rather call her and get advice before driving to Winchester or Cumberland to the Emergency Room.

Since Stacy was a certified Emergency Medical Technician, the state and the handful of local doctors turned a blind eye to her medical advice giving. Oftentimes it cleared the waiting rooms for real emergencies. She practiced common sense caring and never overstepped the bounds of her knowledge. She never prescribed medicine, unless it was an herbal tea or poultice like her grandmothers used up until their deaths. Even those were sanctioned by the older doctors in the area.

"Have a great day. See you this afternoon, right?"

"Yes, ma'am." Remi laid back down until she heard her father's step on the stairs.

She popped out of bed and pulled her knee-length night-gown back down where it belonged. When she heard him stop outside her door she called, "Good morning, Dad. I'm up," before he had a chance to knock.

"Are you sure?" Chance sounded suspicious.

Remi opened the door and poked her head out. "Yes, I'm sure. I'll be out as soon as I get dressed." She closed the door and turned to her closet. A moment later she heard her father heading toward the kitchen.

ॐ

"So, Mr. Christopher," Stacy said after disinfecting Winston's cuts and bruises. She began wrapping a bandage around the chest that was already turning a rainbow of colors. "What the hell happened? You meet up with a bulldozer?"

"Please, call me Winston. Anyone who's seen me in this condition should be friendly enough to call me by my Christian name. In answer to your question, I believe the three clods should be considered a bulldozer, a garbage truck, and a piledriver. I'm just not sure what to call their father. A mountain is the only thing that comes to mind."

"Oh, you met the Johnsons, did you? Did they leave the Brass Rail in one piece or will I be calling the insurance company this afternoon?"

"The Brass Rail is fine. They followed me out into the street when I refused to rise to the taunts about haircuts and sexual preferences. Two of the brutes held me while their father cut off my braid. When I struggled, they decided they wanted to quote, beat the fag out of me, unquote." Winston relayed the scene quickly. He wanted to move forward, away from the painful incident. He'd dealt with the ignorant and stupid before, but this was the first time he'd been assaulted.

Stacy shook her head as she taped the bandage in place. "How about I try my hand at fixing the damage to your hair?"

"Dear lady, I would be forever in your debt if you could do something, but I don't think gluing my braid back is an option."

"No, but I can trim it so you look more like a business-man and less like a drowned rat."

Winston shrugged, then settled in for a proper haircut. "My head is in your hands."

"So how long will this beauty session take? We've got a ton of work to do and only two days to do it," Jeremy said. The living room looked like a tornado went through a paper factory. He needed some advice, from Stacy as well as Winston. How was he to deal with the challenge of producing and directing and dealing with these children?

"It shouldn't take too long. If you'd like, I could fit you in when I'm done with Winston." Stacy opened the drawer by the sink and pulled out the little silver scissors Dottie had used for years to cut hair. Grabbing a damp towel from the top of the washing machine, she draped it around Winston's shoulders, careful to protect his bandages, then began comb-ing and cutting.

Jeremy settled into the chair in the corner with his notes. By the time Winston's haircut was completed, costumes had been discussed and Jeremy had moved on to sets.

"The crew at the high school is always willing to help a good cause," Stacy said. She combed Winston's hair, admiring the way the strands laid, not a hair falling out of place.

"That's great, but this is a production being held in Winchester. Would they still help?" Jermey asked.

"All we have to do is book the auditorium at the high school and run your production here for two nights. Take it on the road, as they say," Winston offered.

"The Friends of the Library could sell tickets and raise money for the library fund." Stacy picked up on the idea.

"We'll have to see if everyone agrees to the additional performances, but I don't see why not." Jeremy made notes.

They filled Stacy in on the production, then recruited her. She knew where to get what and how to get things done in the short time they had. The only bit of news they left out was who would be dancing the role of Clara. Jeremy didn't lie, he just didn't volunteer the information.

By the time Jeremy and Winston left for rehearsal Thursday afternoon, he felt like he was balancing on top of the eight ball, instead of cowering behind it, waiting to be rolled over.

The only problem they hadn't answered was who would dance the part of Uncle. Jeremy couldn't dance the part and Winston much preferred to stay in the background.

ॐ

"Diane, it's Chance Applewhite. I hear you're looking for a strong, virile, sexy dancer for in your Christmas production. I may be old, but I should be able to perform without tripping over my own feet. Call me if I can help."

Diane played the message back a second time, amazed that Chance would actually volunteer. Stacy must have held a gun to his head to force him to make the offer.

With a sigh, she relaxed deeper into the leather chair she'd bought in college. Chance would be perfect as Uncle, but would Jeremy agree to feature his brother? Were the brothers close enough that Chance would make the offer to Jeremy as well? Had Jeremy told his brother what was taking up so much of his time?

Diane erased the message, then picked up the phone. Using her copy of the rules and regulations Jeremy had written out for the girls, she dialed his number, half hoping a machine would answer.

There was something about his voice that wiped coherent thought from her brain. Or maybe it was that he was so handsome. She wanted to see him succeed in this production, even if that success took him back to New York to the "real" theater world. If he succeeded here, surely he could succeed out there. In New York, he'd have trained performers at his disposal.

Diane returned her attention to the ringing in her ear. Four, five, six rings. Did he not have an answering machine?

"Hello?" Diane jumped when a voice replaced the ringing. She didn't answer until the voice repeated a distracted "Hello?"

"Jeremy? It's Diane," she said. Her mouth went dust dry and her palms grew damp.

"Hi Diane, what's up?"

Diane swallowed hard before asking, "Do we still need an Uncle? I have a man who'd like to help."

"Yes, we do. I also need four or six other adults, men and women. Mostly they'll stand in the background but if need be, they might be called on to square dance."

"Square dance? I have just the group. The local square dance club should have someone willing to help us out."

"Great. If possible, have everyone there tomorrow afternoon. I hope to have a rehearsal schedule done and we can explain the changes we're making to the traditional production." Jeremy said. She heard a sound and figured he was making notes to himself about a square dance.

"I'll see what I can do, boss."

"Diane, I was wondering…"

"Yes?"

"Would you join me for dinner tomorrow night?" Jeremy sounded as if his stomach was clenched in knots. His voice also dropped to just above a whisper.

"Sure. Will Winston and Remi be joining us?"

"No, I thought it would be just the two of us."

"Why Dancemaster, are you asking me out? On a date?" Diane smiled. She wasn't sure if confirming the definition of their outing was for his sake or her own.

"Yes, ma'am, I guess I am," he drawled.

"In that case, I'd be delighted to join you for dinner."

"We won't be dressed for anything fancy, so if you know of somewhere quiet we could go…"

"I know just the place," Diane interrupted. "They serve a great beef dish with fresh rolls right from the oven and a chocolate cake that's sinful."

"Sounds great. I'll see you tomorrow at rehearsal then."

"Tomorrow," Diane agreed before hanging up.

Slipping her feet back into her no-nonsense, low-heeled black pumps, she pushed out of her chair. She retrieved her purse from the bottom desk draw and headed for the door. She had some preparing to do before she joined Jeremy for rehearsal tomorrow. Like bake a cake and put together a beef stew and rolls.

Jeremy's smile stretched wide as he hung up the phone. He ignored the two people watching him like a bug under glass. He returned to his notes until Winston cleared his throat loudly.

"Yes?" He asked, raising his head, his smile blossoming into a full-fledged, ear to ear grin.

"What did she say?" Stacy demanded before Winston could form the question.

"About what?"

"About dinner tomorrow night, you crazy dancer!"

Jeremy glanced from one to the other. They were practically drooling. "Did you know that she's found someone to dance Uncle? She also might be able to come up with square dancers."

"But what did she say about dinner?" Winston demanded.

"She said yes. She even knows a place where we can go in rehearsal clothes," Jeremy said. He stood up and limped from the room. "We'll need to take both cars tomorrow. That way you can bring the girls home."

"Sure thing," Winston said, smiling like the mother hen he was. He'd be glad to chauffeur the girls if it meant his friend would have a chance for romance.

A true believer in romance, Winston watched Jeremy dance right by women who would give their right leg for a chance at him. But he never noticed them. Especially when he was involved with a production. Hopefully, this time would be different.

"Does he have a chance?" Winston asked softly.

"Sure, but Diane's not the type he's used to. She's small town, through and through. Maybe if things go well, he'll stay here instead of returning to the bright lights and big cities," Stacy answered as she carefully pulled the towel from around Winston's shoulders.

"That would be a tragedy for the American theater, but it would probably be the best thing for our friend in there," Winston concurred before picking up the mirror to look at himself.

His hair was short all over with layers that feathered back from his face. The layers disguised his thinning hair and made him look almost young again.

"Oh, my God. I'm gorgeous! At least my hair is. The rest of me is just colorful!" he exclaimed. "I hope your husband knows what a treasure he has in you. If he doesn't, please let me steal you away from him."

"But I thought..." Stacy started to ask, but immediately thought better of it.

"That I'm gay? That doesn't mean I couldn't find a place for you in my life. Maybe as my personal assistant and hairstylist." Winston patted the hands that fluttered at Stacy's waist. "Don't be afraid of the word or the man, my dear. I'm not a thing to be frightened of. I do know how to please women outside the bedroom, even if I am gay. That's why so many of my friends are women." He returned his attention to the mirror. Picking up the comb from the table, he ran it through the short blond strands. "Yes, indeed, I am gorgeous. Mitchell won't know what to think."

"Mitchell?" Stacy asked.

"My partner. He's in London right now doing a show, but promised he'd be back for Christmas. He's been after me for years to cut my hair, but I always refused. I never thought I'd find anyone who could cut it so beautifully. Thank you so much, dear Stacy." Winston brushed a kiss across Stacy's cheek before following Jeremy into the living room. "Jeremy, don't you think Mitchell will love my hair? What do you want for lunch? I heard your stomach growling."

Stacy shook her head in amazement. She cleaned up the mess she'd created then slipped out the back door. Jeremy and Winston were debating how hard to work their cast and wouldn't even miss her.

18

$\mathcal{J}$eremy posted the cast list on the wall inside the auditorium. The girls could check the list, but their parents would not see it. He was determined to avoid a scene unless it was absolutely necessary. When Diane arrived with a group of adults, he asked them to sit with the girls facing the stage. He and Winston had set up a group of chairs for the adults. After allowing the girls a few minutes to check the list and congratulate one another, he climbed the steps to the stage and waited, motionless and silent.

The room grew so quiet he thought he could hear Diane's heartbeat. It could have been his own he was listening to. After all, he was as excited as a schoolboy today. He and Winston had finished the bulk of the preparatory work. Now the performance was about to begin. He glanced over the group before him, noting that Diane had recruited enough adults to form two squares for the square dance.

The only person missing was the man who would dance Uncle. Had she been telling tales about finding a willing dancer? Or was the man running late and would burst in during the story Jeremy was about to begin?

"Diane?" Jeremy said as he carefully lowered himself to sit on the edge of the stage. He could see everyone and they could see him. Eye contact was important, but he needed to sit to keep his knee happy.

"Yes?" Diane approached with a smile.

"Which man is to be Uncle?"

"Uncle?"

"You said you had a dancer who was willing to dance the part of Uncle. Which one is it?" Jeremy motioned with one hand towards the four men sitting in the back of the group of dancers.

Diane turned and glanced around the room. "He's not here. He wasn't sure he could make it. He said he'd be happy to dance, but his job is kind of crazy. I'll talk to him tomorrow if you'd like."

"Will you be able to work with him? Winston can help you, but I'm going to have my hands too full with this crew to pamper a prima donna."

"He's not like that, he's just busy," Diane defended Chance against his brother's accusations. "I'll be happy to work with him, if that's what you want."

"Thanks," Jeremy said. Clearing his throat, he addressed the cast. "You've all had time to check the cast list. Congratulations on earning your roles, and welcome to the first meeting of the Cracked Nut Dance Company."

Immediately several hands went up. Caitlyn didn't look happy. The other girls looked both confused and hopeful.

"Let's get through the next few minutes, then if you still have questions we can discuss them. This is not going to be a traditional version of *The Nutcracker*. My friend Winston Christopher has reworked and updated the story and the dances."

꜅

"That went well for a first rehearsal, don't you think?" Jeremy asked. He turned off the lights in the auditorium, then accepted Diane's hand before following her through the darkened room. There was no karate class tonight and they were to lock up.

"You'd know more about first rehearsals than I do," Diane murmured. The warmth spreading through her from where his warm hand touched hers distracted her.

Once they were in the hall and the door secured, they found themselves confronted by Mrs. Kelly. The five-foot tall, three foot wide woman wore a look that would frighten most thunderclouds into scurrying away.

"Miss Cooper, I understand from some of the parents that you locked the entrances to the auditorium during the rehearsal. Is that true?"

"Yes, Mr. Applewhite feels that the only way to keep parents from disrupting rehearsals is to keep them out." Diane released Jeremy's hand. She took a half step sideways. No need to begin gossip and Mrs. Kelly knew everything that went on within a five-mile radius of the Arts Center.

"That's totally unacceptable. The fire marshall will shut this place down if word reaches him that we're locking children inside rooms with no way to escape in the event of a fire. From now on, you must keep those doors unlocked." Mrs. Kelly bristled, looking like a frowsy, angry little dog.

Jeremy opened his mouth to protest, but Diane touched his arm and stepped in front of him instead. "We're hoping to keep the production a secret for the most part. We don't want the girls to be intimidated by an audience before they're ready. Would you be willing to post a guard here to keep the parents from coming into the auditorium?"

"If it's that important to you, simply tell the parents that the rehearsals are closed , and they'll understand," Mrs. Kelly said.

"I doubt that," Jeremy muttered.

"We'll try that, Mrs. Kelly. I'm sorry about the mix up. We didn't know that we shouldn't lock the doors," Diane said. She reached back and grabbed Jeremy's arm in warning. It wouldn't do their cause any good if he offended this lady.

"Please do not lock the doors any more. We've never had any problems, and I'd rather not have to explain why little girls got burned up if a fire broke out," Mrs. Kelly continued to scold, following Jeremy and Diane to the parking lot doors.

"Why did you pacify her like that?" Jeremy grumbled once they were outside.

"We need her on our side if we're going to use the dance room as well as the auditorium for the next couple of weeks. Besides, it *is* against the law to lock those doors. We'll just have to post a sign that we're running closed rehearsals."

"Fine. The first parent who comes through those doors will be shot," Jeremy vowed. He unlocked the car, then threw his bag into the back. "Now, enough talk of the unpleasant Pekingese lady. Where are we going for dinner?"

"Do you trust me?" she asked as they settled in the car.

"Should I?"

"Of course you should. But I'm asking if you trust me to drive your car?"

Jeremy swallowed before answering. "Uh, yeah, I guess. Just be careful with her, okay?"

"Close your eyes," she ordered as they left the parking lot.

"Close my eyes?" Jeremy asked, looking at her with one eyebrow cocked.

"Yes, close your eyes. And keep them closed until I tell you." Diane stopped the car at a red light. She turned her head to meet his gaze.

She was up to something, but if he didn't know yet what

it was. "Oh, all right. Drive on, McDuff." With that, Jeremy closed his eyes and lifted both hands to cover his face.

"And no peeking."

"Of course not. I'd hate to ruin your surprise."

Jeremy took a deep breath and bit the inside of his cheek when she hit the gas and rapidly sped up, turning first to the left, then quickly to the right. She drove and drove, stopping and turning randomly until Jeremy was completely lost. Finally, the car stopped and she turned off the engine.

"You can open your eyes now," she said softly.

Jeremy took down his hands, then blinked several times to focus his eyes. He looked around, but they weren't in a restaurant parking lot. They were behind a house. A big, gray, stone house. There were cars parked nearby, but that didn't tell him where they were.

"Welcome to my home," she said when he turned to her.

༄

The first rehearsal went better than Winston could have hoped for. After they'd heard the music, the square dancing adults claimed they had a routine that would go with it. They took a copy of the music tape and promised to perform it for Jeremy's approval in two weeks. Once the adults had been dismissed Jeremy, Winston, and Diane turned their attention to the girls. After breaking them into the three groups that would perform the chorus numbers together, Diane demonstrated the steps while Jeremy called the sequences.

The girls quickly picked up their steps. From their whispers, they seemed excited about the dances. They left tired, happy, and looking forward to Saturday's rehearsal.

On the way home, Winston wanted to sing, but Remi was obviously distressed about something. Instead of bouncing with joy at being chosen for the lead, she sat silent, lost in thought. She barely responded to Marcie's excited chatter, so the other girl drifted into silence as well. After Marcie climbed out at her house, Winston drove on, his remaining passenger silent.

"Could you drop me off at the restaurant tonight, Mr. Winston?" She broke her silence as they approached the turn to her house.

"Certainly, my dear. Any special reason?" Winston asked. He hoped she would share whatever was causing her to be so somber.

"I'm going tell my dad about the ballet."

"You're not going to keep it a surprise?"

"No, it's too hard keeping secrets. My mom suspects something already. I figure I'll tell Dad so he won't feel left out. I'll tell Mom when I get home." Remi slumped down further into her seat. "I hope they don't make me quit," she whispered just loud enough for Winston to hear.

"Why ever would they do that? You're a dancer, aren't you? This production will give you the opportunity to show off the talent that runs strong and deep in your family."

"I'm supposed to be on restriction. I'm not sure dancing in Winchester is allowed while I'm on restriction, even if I am with you and Uncle Jeremy."

"You are mostly working with Jeremy, so your parents shouldn't have anything to complain about." Winston pulled to a halt in front of the Brass Rail. "Here you go, Dancer. Safe and sound."

Remi smiled. When Winston called her Dancer it made her feel warm and grown up. When T.J. used the same nickname, she felt like she had to defend her love of the art.

"Thanks, Mr. Winston. Do you want to come inside?

Maybe Dad won't get so angry if you're there when I talk to him."

"Thanks for the vote of confidence, but I'm not sure your dad would like to see me quite yet."

"All right. See you Saturday," Remi said. She reached over the seat to grab her school backpack and dance bag from the back seat.

Winston waited until she entered the restaurant before putting the car into gear. A peanut butter sandwich and some canned soup would suffice for dinner. Tomorrow he would put together something they could eat on the fly.

19

*R*emi stepped in the front door of the Brass Rail and scanned the open room. Her dad was nowhere in sight. He must be in his office muttering over the paperwork that seemed to multiply if he ignored it for more than two days.

"Hi, Remi," Toby North said as he pushed a cart of dirty dishes toward the kitchen.

"Hi, Toby. Is my dad in back?"

"No, he's at the courthouse meeting with the planning commission. They're trying to decide what to do with the empty lot next door."

"Oh," Remi said, wondering if the courage to share her secret would last long enough for her father to return. "Do you know if he's coming back?"

"I don't know, but let's go ask Sherry. She'll know." Toby motioned for her to precede him into the back of the building. Remi sat at her table to wait until Sherry, the assistant manager and head cook, had a moment to talk to her. Toby turned his cart over to the dishwasher, then visited the daily special station.

"Eat that," he ordered, setting an overflowing plate in front of her.

"All of it?" Remi eyes widened. Ribs filled more than half the plate and roasted new potatoes covered the rest.

"At least try," he said, handing her a white cotton hand

towel to wipe her fingers on. "You're so skinny, you'll blow away during the first storm of winter."

"Thank you, I think." Remi took his criticism as a complement. Dancers were supposed to be thin.

"I was wondering if you'd like to go to the Halloween Hop with me," Toby asked long moments later. He'd inhaled his meal while she'd barely touched hers.

Remi stared at him over the rib she was delicately nibbling on. "Excuse me?"

"The Halloween Hop. Would you like to go with me?" Toby restated the question. He tried not to sound impatient, though the wait was eating a hole in his gut.

Remi remained silent with a rib held between sauce-covered fingers as she turned the invitation over in her mind. "I'd like that, but I'll have to check with Dad first."

"He said it was okay, as long as I have you home before midnight and I guarantee that no one in the car will be drinking anything stronger than soda. Oh yeah, he also made me promise not to have anything to do with T.J. Frederickson. Why would he ask that?" Toby picked a rib off her plate and began gnawing on it.

Remi had to smile. Her father had nothing to worry about. Toby was very different than T.J. "Probably because T.J.'s gotten me in trouble a couple of times lately. Why did you ask my dad before you asked me?" Remi asked.

"I was trying to figure out how to ask you earlier and he overheard me practicing. I had to tell him when he demanded to know what was going on."

"You were worried about asking me?" Remi asked. She was amazed that Toby would confess to such a thing.

"Yeah. I wasn't sure you'd want to be seen with me."

"I'd like to go to the dance with you, Toby. I'd like that a lot."

His confessions turned Remi's thoughts to her own planned confession to her father. She would have to put it on hold for a while. Would she be able to keep the secret for the six weeks until the first performance? Should she try?

"You okay?" Toby asked. He touched her hand. "You look really intense."

"I'm trying to figure out if I should tell my dad something or keep it a secret for a while longer," Remi softly.

"What kind of secret?" Toby took her hand and wiped each finger free of barbecue sauce.

"I went to Winchester and tried out for the Christmas production when I wasn't supposed to." Remi said. Her stomach was doing funny things as Toby wiped her hands clean. Suddenly her skin felt too small for her body.

"Did you get a part?"

"I'm playing Clara, the lead," Remi said, meeting Toby's eyes.

"That's great! Why wouldn't you want to tell your dad? He's really a great guy." Toby continued to hold her hand.

"I'm on restriction. I wasn't supposed to go to the auditions. But Uncle Jeremy said that since he was with me it would be okay. I went, but the director was hurt in a car accident and Uncle Jeremy had to take over, so I auditioned and found out today that I'm going to dance the lead. Winston says he's never seen anyone my age as good as me, and he's a choreographer in New York City."

"Sounds like you're going to be dancing on Broadway before too long." Toby said.

"So the question of the evening is whether or not I should tell my dad."

"Tell your dad what?" Chance overheard the question, his approach masked by the noise from the kitchen.

Remi paused a moment before answering. Her secret would have to wait. "That I'm going with Toby to the Halloween Hop in two weeks."

"Oh, yeah? That's great! So what can I do for you tonight? Your mom's teaching and I've got to close tonight." Chance asked. He'd promised Toby he wouldn't let on that he'd already given his permission for the date.

"I was hoping for a ride home, but I guess I'll walk up to the studio and see if Mom's still there." Remi stood, wiping her hands one last time on one of the thick terrycloth towels the restaurant used as napkins.

"Toby can take you home," Chance said as he dug into his pocket for the keys to his truck.

"I can?" Toby asked. No one drove Chance's truck, but he was handing the keys to the busboy who'd only been working for him for a couple of weeks.

"Yeah, just get back here when you're done. There's a Thursday night football game on ESPN and we'll be busy." Chance turned and strolled away. He fought the urge to turn back and see what happened next.

"Well, I guess I have a ride home. Come on." Remi grabbed Toby's hand and led him through the kitchen and out the back door where her father parked his truck.

As they passed through the storeroom, Toby pulled off his apron. He grabbed his coat from the rack next to the back door. It was cooling off quickly at night, even though the old people around town were exclaiming that it was the warmest fall any of them could remember. As he opened the passenger door for Remi, he wondered if Chance would time the trip to the Applewhite house.

Once they were out of town, Remi's stomach clenched. What would happen when they reached the house? Would

Toby insist on a goodnight kiss? In case he wanted a kiss, Remi ran her tongue over her teeth and prayed she didn't have anything stuck between them. Glancing toward her driver, she allowed herself to daydream about exactly what kissing Toby would be like.

The closer the truck got to her house, the more nervous Remi became. Without her parents at home, what would Toby do? She was so lost in thought that when Toby turned off the engine, she jumped. Looking around, she couldn't believe they'd reached the house already. Eyes wide, she turned to Toby and waited for his next move.

Only he didn't make one. He just sat and stared at her in the dim light of the dashboard. The silence grew so strained, Remi was certain the air would splinter around them, leaving a silent vacuum behind.

"What?" Remi finally asked. She hoped she didn't have a smear of barbecue sauce on her cheek. She raised a hand to her cheek but didn't feel anything sticky. Why was Toby staring at her?

"You're just so pretty," Toby finally replied. "When you finish growing up, you're going to be dynamite."

Remi felt her cheeks heat under his steady stare. Ducking her head, she studied the fingers knotted together in her lap. "You don't have to say things like that. I know I'm too skinny and flat-chested and…"

"You're perfect," Toby broke in. The thread of steel in his voice caused Remi to raise her head and look at him.

Only he wasn't looking in her direction. He stared straight ahead, out the windshield. His expression was grim. Like he was kicking himself for voicing his opinion. His hands gripped the steering wheel, as if he needed the grounding the circle provided.

Remi laid her left hand over his right one where it gripped the wheel. "You look like you're having some intense thoughts."

"You could say that. I was wondering how soon I could ask you to marry me," Toby stated bluntly. He still didn't look in her direction.

"Marry you? I'm only sixteen years old."

"I'm sixteen too, and I've loved you since I was six. I hate it when you go off with T.J. and his friends. I don't want you doing it any more, okay?"

"He's just a friend, Toby."

"He says he's more than just a friend. He says he's going to marry you as soon as you're old enough to support him." Toby said. He turned to her, his expression tortured and his eyes haunted. "I love you, Remi Applewhite. I know we're too young, but I want you to marry me when you decide the time is right."

His intentions clearly stated, Toby reached out, unsnapped Remi's seatbelt and pulled her across the seat, turning so he met her face to face, lips to lips, and chest to chest. His arms slipped around her to cradle her close.

Taken by surprise, Remi didn't react instantly. Then she tried to figure out what to do with her hands that lay against his chest. Pushing out of his arms didn't feel right.

His kiss was perfect. His lips were warm and firm. He didn't try to stick his tongue in her mouth.

After a moment, Toby pulled back, breathing hard. "Kiss me back," he murmured. Then he closed the gap between them again.

Remi tried to respond but didn't know what to do. Whenever T.J. kissed her, she paid more attention to fighting her way out of his embrace than kissing him. Tonight, she wanted to kiss Toby back. But there was a shiver of fear at what came next.

When Toby's tongue stroked her lips, she turned her head and pushed away. "I'm sorry, but I'm not ready for this," she said. She'd tried the same approach with T.J., but maybe Toby would be different and not throw a temper tantrum.

Taking a deep breath, he allowed her to slide away from him. "Thank you," he said hoarsely.

"For what? I said no," Remi said.

"It's the fact that you did say no. You're a strong woman who knows what you want. I just hope in the years to come that you'll still want me in your life." Toby said. He knew that baring his soul wouldn't work with most of the girls, but Remi was different. Hopefully, being completely honest was the right thing to do.

Remi didn't know how to respond. "I'll always want you in my life, Toby. But for now, could we keep the fact that you want to marry me a secret. If my father knew…"

"He'd blow a gasket." Toby finished her sentence for her.

"Besides, you may change your mind by the time I graduate from high school," Remi smiled. The warm glow in her center burned bright but not terrifyingly out of control.

"Then I guess we'll just have to go steady for a while and see what happens from there. How does that sound?" Toby said. His lips curved in a smile, though his body shivered.

Remi thought for a moment, then nodded. "I'd like that. I guess I'd better go in so you can get back to work."

"Yeah, I guess. Otherwise you're dad's gonna be suspicious that something more went on than was supposed to."

Remi leaned across the seat and brushed a quick kiss across his lips. Then she opened the door and slid out before he could react. Once on the ground, she glanced back into the truck. "I'll see you."

"You can count on that," Toby replied with a grin.

Remi raced to the house and let herself in before she gave into the impulse to climb back into the truck and accept Toby's marriage proposal. She was only sixteen years old! Her life lay ahead of her, an uncharted land with a multitude of paths yet untried. It was way too soon to plan her life yet. She needed to focus on Mr. Turkle's history examination on Tuesday and a heavy rehearsal schedule for the next six weeks. And the Halloween Hop. She had a date for the Halloween Hop.

Toby waited until the front door closed behind her, then started the truck and left the driveway. He was tempted to stop, get out and do a dance himself, but a glance at the clock on the dashboard told him Chance would be questioning his delay already. He settled for whistling a happy tune to express the joy in his heart. Remi hadn't laughed at his proposal. She hadn't told him no, and she'd even agreed to go steady with him!

Always a worrier, Toby began to wonder what going steady would entail. With her dancing and his job and their studies, there wouldn't be a lot of time for dating and fooling around. But there was the Halloween Hop and the Christmas formal and maybe they'd be able to fit in a drive to Cumberland or Winchester for a movie. They'd figure it out as they went along. For now, he had to get back to work before Chance came looking for him.

20

"I'm sorry Jeremy, but Chance isn't here. He's out of town helping a friend. Can I help?" Stacy smiled while Jeremy cursed in her ear. She didn't tell him that he was the friend being helped.

"Is he mad at me, Stacy? Did I piss him off and not realize it? I've been trying to get together with him for three weeks."

"And he's been trying to get together with you. It seems like you've been running opposite schedules. Shall I tell him you called?"

"Yeah, same message as the last twelve times I've called." Jeremy hung up before swearing again.

It surprised him how much not being able to talk to Chance bothered him. Before returning to Romney, he hadn't spoken with his brother for seventeen years. He'd been back in town almost two months, but he'd settled in. He was even beginning to feel indispensable—at least to twenty-five teenagers and a dancing attorney. His days had fallen into a routine of physical therapy and rehearsals. His evenings were spent learning about Diane's life, wants, needs, and dreams.

With the restaurant, the dance studio, and his family, Chance was just as busy, but Jeremy wondered about his helping a friend. He'd been doing that a lot the last couple of weeks. He'd have to corner Chance and find out exactly what was going on.

Picking the phone up again, he tried Diane's office. But she wasn't in either. The elderly woman who acted as her secretary during office hours said Diane was out, and she wasn't certain when she'd be returning.

"Well, damn. Everybody has somewhere to be but me," Jeremy muttered as he hung up the phone. He pushed out of the kitchen chair and made his way to the back porch.

It was cooler now than it had been when he'd arrived in town. The leaves were falling from the trees like flame-colored rain. Halloween was only a few days away. He'd have to buy some candy for the kids who would surely come trick or treating.

Gazing across the back yard at Mrs. Cannady's two hundred-year-old oaks, Jeremy wondered what he could do to fill the empty hours. Even Winston was busy, entertaining the Hampshire County High School drama department with a series of lectures on Broadway and the truth about life as an actor, choreographer, and director.

Bending his knee, Jeremy was grateful the pain was easing. All it took was lots of rest and limited use. The swelling was down and the bruising had finally faded. The limp was almost gone, but his dancing days were over. It was just as well.

He'd performed every part he'd ever dreamt of. It was time to step aside for younger, more agile dancers. It was time to make the formal announcement of his retirement. Then he'd have to figure of what to do for the next fifty years or so. He refused to make commercials endorsing floor wax or pantyhose or some other nonsense as other dancers and athletes had done.

He wanted to direct, to create, to continue what he was doing now. He liked putting together this production with a non-existent budget. He got charged up watching the girls learn their parts and seeing how their individuality would become part of the whole production. All he had to do was figure out how to finance such a company without returning to the city. He wanted to stay here and live in this place of quiet nights and slow pace. He wanted to stay in the same house for years and not worry about redecorating every spring.

"Right now, you lazy bum, it's time to clean the house before the place is condemned by the Health Department," he said to himself.

He and Winston hadn't cleaned since moving in. The dust was building up on Dottie's bric-a-brac. The kitchen floor crunched every time he walked across it. He had the whole day to himself and he was going to spend it cleaning. What an exciting life he led, he thought. He opened the tiny closet by the back door and pulled out the vacuum cleaner.

⁓

"Winston, do we have to go straight back to Romney?" Remi asked the Tuesday before Halloween.

"Why? Do you have plans?"

"I was wondering if we could stop at the mall and go shopping."

"Shopping?"

"The Halloween Hop is Friday and I need to find a dress that will knock Toby's socks off," Remi explained simply. "I have money from working for Uncle Jeremy. I just need to find a dress. There's not enough time to order from a catalog and there is nothing in Romney."

"Toby? I thought your boyfriend was that T.J. person," Winston asked.

"Every time I go out with T.J., he does something to get

me in trouble. Now that I'm finally off restriction, I'm going to stay away from him. So can we please go shopping for a dress?"

"I don't see why not. I'll even buy you dinner before we hit the stores." Winston said. "My only requirement is that I get to help pick out this dress that has to knock Toby's socks off."

"That sounds terrific!"

As Winston drove, he visualized the perfect dress for the young dancer beside him. Something light, floaty, but not too short or too low cut. She was sixteen, a mere baby in the grand scheme of life.

෴

"What exactly is going on between you and Toby?" Winston asked over a dinner of chef salads and hot rolls at the Sweet Apple Café.

"We're uh, just friends, I guess," Remi said. She studied her salad closely before stabbing a cherry tomato with her fork.

"You guess? Don't you know? After all, you're buying a new dress in order to knock his socks off, aren't you?"

"Can you keep a secret?" Remi raised her eyes to meet Winston's curious gaze.

"I've been known to keep a secret or two in my time. You're not married to Toby or anything like that, are you?" Winston asked, horrified at such a thought.

"No! Of course not! But Toby did propose."

"Propose what?"

"Propose marriage," Remi said slowly.

"You're too young to get married!" Winston stated loudly. People at the tables around them glanced their way, more interested in the conversation at their table than their own.

"I know I'm too young. I told Toby I wouldn't think about marriage until I at least graduated from high school. It will be even longer if I can find a way to get accepted into the performing arts high school I want to go to."

"Thank God. I'd hate to have my plans shot down because you're in love." Winston relaxed deeper into his chair.

"Your plans? What plans?"

Winston remained silent as he cut a roll in half and spread honey butter across its steaming center.

"If all goes well, I was going to offer to sponsor you at the New York High School for the Performing Arts. Then I'd introduce you to a couple of people who could put you to work as a dancer. But you have to stay single and sober and off drugs," he stated flatly.

"Really? That would be fantastic. But they turned me down a couple of months ago. I don't have enough production experience, and I don't live in New York City." Remi couldn't stop her eyes from growing wide or her heart racing with excitement.

"A few more rehearsals and you'll qualify as a professional. And I know a woman who might be talked into providing room and board to a bright rising star. But you're going to have to dance your heart out from now until Christmas."

"You won't tell my dad that Toby proposed, will you?" Remi asked. "Dad would go nuts if he knew. He might even fire him, and Toby really needs his job."

"Don't worry. I'll keep your secret, if you keep mine. I don't want your father and uncle to hunt me down because I've set your sights on something bigger than Hampshire County High School and a life hiding in these mountains."

"Deal!" Remi held out her hand and smiled when Win-

ston shook it. "Am I really good enough to think about going
to New York?"

"Yes, Dancer, you really are good enough. So don't go
accepting any proposals, okay?"

"Yes, sir."

"So, where do you want to begin the search for this dress?"
Winston left several bills on the table next to their check,
then led Remi to the main expanse of the mall.

"Mom and I usually shop at Penney's down that way," she
pointed to their right, "or we go to Sears which is down there,"
she pointed to their left.

Winston shuddered at the thought of putting this delicate young woman in an ordinary dress from a nationwide
chain. He wished he had time to call one of his friends in
New York for the dress of his vision. But that would take too
long.

She was meant for a designer dress that would accentuate
her delicate build while not putting her on display for everyone to ogle. The dress should also be one she could wear at
Christmas and maybe even the prom next spring.

"Let's wander on down toward Penney's and see what we
can find," he said. He held out his arm and smiled when
Remi took it with a grin. He'd never imagined himself in the
role of fairy godfather, but here he was, escorting a teenager
Cinderella on a shopping spree.

They looked in the store windows, discussing the clothes
they saw, amazed that the red and green Christmas decora-
tions were already battling with the orange and black of Halloween.

A flash of color caught Winston's eye. He turned and
froze when he focused on it. There it was: the perfect dress.
Exactly what he'd imagined. The small storefront had three

dresses in the window, one black, one silver, and the third the pastel rainbow that Winston immediately saw Remi wearing Friday night.

"Come on, Dancer," he said. He guided Remi across the mall toward the dress. His focus was so fixed on that store window, he almost ran over a pair of gray-haired ladies who were power-walking the mall.

"What? Winston, where are we going?"

"I've found the dress, the perfect dress. What size are you?" Winston nodded toward the storefront. He didn't release her until they were inside the store.

"Six, I think," Remi paused when he released her.

Approaching the sales counter, Winston met the eyes of the two salesclerks who were describing in graphic detail their previous evening's activities. They were high school students with too much—too much makeup, too much cloying perfume, and too many holes in each ear with cheap earrings.

"Excuse me, I'd like to see the dress in the window in a size six, please."

The pair half turned their backs to him. They seemed to be of the mind that if they could not see him, he was not there.

Winston had run into such ignorance before, but he refused to put up with it this time. These two didn't make the first cut when it came to ignorant homophobic behavior.

"Excuse me? Where is your manager?" Winston raised the volume of his voice while dropping the tone. The two other women in the store turned to stare as he made his stand.

"Why?" The taller of the two turned and cocked her head to stare down her nose at him.

"I was wondering if she knew how rude her clerks were to her customers," Winston said. He didn't notice an older woman enter the store until she laid a hand on his arm.

"May I help you, sir?" She asked softly.

"Are you the manager?"

"Yes, I'm Mrs. James, the night manager. What can I help you with this evening?" One stern look from her and the sales clerks went scurrying.

"I wondered if you had that dress in the window in a size six." Winston nodded toward the front window.

"Which dress, sir?"

"The rainbow dress," Winston elaborated on his choice. "Remi, come here," he called to the girl, who was looking through sweaters on the sale table.

Mrs. James glanced from the girl to the dress in the window and nodded. "Yes, it would be perfect and I do believe we do have a size six."

Thirty minutes later, Remi and Winston left the mall. Remi carried the dress draped over both forearms like a baby. Winston carried two bags, one containing shoes and the other, a featherweight shawl.

"Thank you Winston! This dress is so beautiful, Toby won't know what to think!"

"I just hope your dad doesn't come after me for contributing to the maturity of a sixteen year old," Winston joked. He helped her put their purchases in the back seat of the car.

"Don't worry, I'll protect you," Remi assured him.

"Now can we go home? Shopping with you is exhausting," Winston teased.

"Exhausted already? How would you handle shopping with a true shopaholic?"

"I'd never go shopping with her. That's why I catalog shop. With a phone call and a credit card, my wardrobe's on the way."

"Home, Winston," Remi giggled as she settled back in her seat.

Winston sent the car westward. Being a fairy godfather felt great. Remi would be a vision in her new dress. He only hoped Toby knew the future she could have. For now, he'd keep her secret. But if Toby made any moves beyond a goodnight kiss or two, Winston would break his pledge of secrecy and spill the beans to Chance and Jeremy. Then he'd sit back and watch the fireworks.

21

Every other Thursday, Diane and Stacy got together for lunch at the Brass Rail. They always sat in the back booth and ate and giggled and enjoyed each other's company.

"So have you told Chance who he's dancing for yet?" Stacy asked Diane the Thursday before Halloween.

"He hasn't asked, so I haven't bothered to tell him that I'm not the director. How about you? Have you told Jeremy who his mysterious 'Uncle' is?"

Stacy scanned the menu at the Brass Rail. "Not yet. It's been a challenge keeping those two apart. I think Jeremy is beginning to suspect something. The last time I talked to him, he asked me about this friend Chance has been helping out. He wanted to know exactly who the friend was and whether I trusted this friend or not. I believe he's come to the conclusion that Chance is having an affair."

The two women giggled at the silliness of that thought.

"Another couple of weeks and the secrets will be revealed," Diane said. "The production will run its course and there won't be anything holding Jeremy here. He'll go for his knee surgery, then get his career back on track." Diane's voice dropped. "He'll be back in the big time and won't have time for this small town lawyer and part-time dance teacher."

"You don't know that," Stacy patted Diane's hand. "He may decide he likes small town life and loves a certain dancing lawyer who shall remain nameless."

"Sure. He'd give up fame, fortune, and Broadway. Not for me and a group of girls whose parents are beginning to wonder if there really will be a production," said Diane.

"Why's that?"

"Jeremy refuses to allow anyone in the rehearsal hall but the cast and crew. He says it's to keep the stage mothers from giving him an ulcer."

"Makes sense to me. I'll have to try that when we're getting ready for recitals next month. That way the girls can focus on learning their steps instead of showing off for the audience. Is he going to open the dress rehearsals?"

"I think so, but only after we've got everything working right. Enough about me. How are you and Remi and Chance?"

"Fine. Remi has a date tomorrow night, but she refuses to go shopping for something to wear. She says she's already got her dress and that it will knock her date's socks off."

"How did she get a dress without you taking her shopping?"

Stacy stabbed at her salad. "She and Winston went shopping Tuesday, but she won't show me the dress. She says I'll have to wait until tomorrow to see it."

"You don't think it's one of those micro mini-dresses that's hardly there, do you?"

"No. I trust Winston to steer her away from trashy," Stacy sipped her coffee. She glanced over Diane's shoulder and her smile widened. "Hey there, stranger. What are you doing here?"

Jeremy stopped by the table and leaned over to kiss Stacy on her cheek. Then he turned and kissed Diane full on the lips. "Hey there, you."

"Hi yourself. What's up?" Diane slid over to make room for him next to her on the seat.

He settled in and waved off the waitress who'd been headed in his direction.

"Your secretary told me you were here, so I thought I'd come by and say hello. I thought maybe I'd catch Chance here, but Monica tells me he won't be in until later. Something about an appointment or something," Jeremy grumbled, disgruntled that he still wasn't able to catch up with his brother.

"Speaking of appointments, I have one in just a few minutes," Diane glanced at her watch. "I'm sorry, but I really must be off."

Jeremy stood, letting her escape from the booth. She laid a bill on the table to cover her meal, then raced from the restaurant as if a monster were chasing her.

"Wow! She must be running late," Stacy returned to pick at the remnants of her salad.

"Funny, her secretary didn't say anything about any appointments this afternoon," Jeremy frowned as he watched Diane cross the street to her car.

"Maybe it's something she didn't tell Alma about," Stacy tried to assure her brother-in-law. "For a secretary, Alma isn't known to keep secrets."

"Yeah, I guess. How are the sets and ticket sales going?" He turned back to the table only after Diane's car drove out of sight.

"Everything is going fine. The sets will be delivered two weeks from Saturday, right on schedule. Ticket sales are going well. We should have a full house for both performances."

"As soon as we have the sets in place, we'll begin dress rehearsals. Were you and Winston able to put together the list of clothing each girl will have to provide?" Jeremy jotted a quick note on a paper napkin, then stuffed it in his pocket.

They continued discussing the preparations until Stacy

finished her lunch. Then he headed to Winchester for his therapy session and Stacy went to the grocery store.

❧

"What do you mean you can't rehearse this afternoon? We were going to go over the *pas de deux* one last time before moving on to your solo." Jeremy stared at his niece as if she'd grown a second head and was turning purple.

As was his Friday afternoon habit, he met Remi and Marcie at Dottie's house before they headed to the dance studio. After an extended rehearsal session, he took the girls to the Brass Rail for a late supper. Then he returned them home. But today Marcie hadn't shown, and now Remi was telling him she couldn't stay.

"I'm sorry, Uncle Jeremy, but I have a date tonight for the Halloween Hop at school."

"Who's your date?" Jeremy narrowed his eyes as he studied her. "It's not that T.J. person, is it? I won't let you go out with him, no matter what your parents say."

"No, it's not T.J. My date is Toby North. He's sixteen and works at the Brass Rail. Mom and Dad said it was okay," Remi explained quickly. She had to get to the Clip and Curl for her appointment.

Over the last several weeks Jeremy had become as protective as her parents. "Marcie and I are both going out tonight. We'll be happy to rehearse extra tomorrow," she blurted out. Why couldn't she and Toby go out on one simple date without everyone nosing into their business?

"Be home early. We're going over the entire second act tomorrow," Jeremy sighed. The girl was right.

Just because he was single-minded about the production didn't mean everyone else was. She was young and should be going to dances and out with boys. She needed a life beyond the theater; otherwise she'd end up like him—old and alone and scared.

"Thanks, Uncle Jeremy. I'll see you tomorrow!" Remi danced out the door and ran the two blocks to the beauty parlor. She arrived two minutes before her appointment time. She planned on wowing Toby with the beautiful dress that made her look older and a new hairstyle and even a manicure. She tap-danced in her sneakers as she waited for Wanda the Curl Queen's attentions.

~

Three hours later, Remi took a deep breath as she reached for her bedroom doorknob. She was dressed and wore the minimal amount of makeup allowed by her parents. For this moment she looked sophisticated and grown up. That afternoon, after a long overdue trim, Wanda, the queen of curl, pulled her hair back into a fancy French braid Remi would never have managed on her own.

The Halloween Hop had an unusual dress code; participants could either attend wearing an easily recognizable costume, or semi-formal attire. She and Toby had opted to dress up. Neither of them had the time to put a proper costume together.

So there she was staring at herself in the full-length mirror, afraid to turn the knob and step from the safety of her bedroom. Maybe Toby wouldn't show up. Then what would she do?

A knock on the door startled her. She jumped back, twisted the knob, and pulled the door open with her.

"Honey, Toby's here," Stacy said as she poked her head through the open door. She spoke before looking at her daughter. "Oh, my."

Remi released the doorknob and stepped back, waiting for her mother's next words. "Oh my" was either a really good thing or a really bad thing, depending on what the next words out of her mother's mouth were.

When she didn't say anything, Remi spun around once then blurted out, "Well? Is it too ugly or too dressy or just too?"

"You're beautiful, honey. Just beautiful. So grown up and yet still very much my little girl," Stacy said. She stepped into the room and carefully gathered her daughter close for a hug that wouldn't wrinkle her. "You and Winston did this?"

"It was mostly Winston. He saw the dress and talked me into trying it on. Then he told me I had to buy this dress or else," Remi replied. She hugged her mother for a moment before pulling away and slowly twirled. The layers floated up, then settled around her once again when she stopped spinning.

"Your father's going to have a fit," Stacy smiled, "but don't listen to him. He's just an overprotective father. A father who doesn't want to admit that the little girl he used to dance with in the middle of the night is all grown up. Come on, Toby's waiting."

Remi picked up her shawl and followed her mother. She paused just before entering the living room. Butterflies the size of dinner plates were flying around her stomach. Toby and her father were talking softly out of sight.

Taking a deep breath, Remi took two steps forward. But they didn't notice her entrance. They were too busy. A soccer game played on the television.

"Go! Go! Yeah!" Chance bounced in his seat as his team scored.

Remi crossed behind the couch, but they ignored her.

Clearing her throat, she hoped for some response. The sound was drowned out by the crowd going wild over the goal that tied the score in the last two minutes of the game.

When things settled down on screen, she leaned forward, putting one hand on her father's shoulder and one on Toby's. "Dad, if you'll give me your truck keys, I'll leave you two alone and go to the dance by myself."

The men turned at the same time, then jumped to their feet.

"Oh, wow!" Toby murmured, straightening the jacket of his borrowed navy blue suit. It was a bit long in the sleeves and legs, but tight around the middle. At least his pants wouldn't fall down.

"Oh, wow, indeed! You're beautiful, honey! Just beautiful," Chance rounded the sofa, then took her hand and spun her in a circle.

"Oh, wow!" Toby repeated. His brain went blank as to what would be the proper thing to say next.

"Thanks, Toby," Remi said, suddenly shy and uncertain.

"I guess we'd better get going if we're going to stop by and see Winston before the dance," Toby said as he came around the sofa, careful to pick his feet up. He wasn't used to wearing dress shoes and had already slipped in them a couple of times.

"Have fun, you two," Stacy called from the kitchen where she was watching the popcorn pop in the microwave.

"Be home by eleven," Chance said, crossing his arms and trying to look stern.

"Daddy! Twelve, okay?"

"All right, but remember, no drinking and no funny business," he squinted his eyes a bit, frowning in Toby's direction.

"Yes, sir. No, sir. Twelve o'clock, sir. We'll be here, sir."

Toby swallowed hard under the glare.

"Bye, Daddy. Bye, Mom."

"Have fun!" Stacy called, leaning into the living room.

"Just not too much!" Chance ordered.

Remi allowed herself to be whisked from the house and into Toby's father's pickup truck without another word. They were halfway to town when she finally broke the heavy silence in the truck. "Do I look okay, Toby?"

"You look fantastic. You'll be the prettiest girl at the dance," Toby responded, reaching over and taking her hand in his.

His palms were sweating, but she needed his reassurance. He needed to feel her skin. When skin touched skin his blood pressure rose and he began breathing high in his chest. Thank goodness for seatbelts. Otherwise he'd pull her close and start kissing her and they'd never make it to the dance. But first a quick drive through town to see Winston, the man responsible for creating this beauty sitting beside him.

〜

"I knew that dress would be perfect." Winston gushed as he circled the young couple in the living room. "Isn't she beautiful, Jeremy?"

Jeremy stared a long time before answering. "Yes, she is, very beautiful. Enjoy your date, but don't forget we have a full run through tomorrow. We'll pick you up at ten o'clock. Don't stay out too late," Jeremy said as he eyed her silent escort. He wasn't sure he liked the young man in the ill-fitting suit. He looked both protective of and in awe of the young woman by his side. His expression said that this evening was about more than just a dance.

"Yes, Monsieur Director," Remi said as she kissed her uncle

on the cheek. She took Toby's hand and led him from the house.

After the truck pulled from the driveway and headed toward the high school, Winston settled on the couch with the latest copy of *Variety*. "They're a good looking couple," he said casually.

"He's too old for her. I can't believe you helped her pick out that dress," Jeremy grumbled. He turned on the television and flipped through the five channels the antenna brought in before turning it off again.

"He's the same age, sixteen, just taller and more mature looking. I helped her because she asked me to. One year may seem like a lot now, but in a few years that difference will be nothing. Just think, someday that boy could be your nephew," Winston said. The possibility caused Jeremy's gut to clench.

"No way. She's got a promising future away from these mountains. I want her to see the world before settling down to be a busboy's wife." Jeremy said through gritted teeth.

"I have an idea about that. Would you be okay with me calling in a favor or two in your name? It might be good for both you and Remi."

"What kind of favor?"

"The kind of favor that could set you up with a new career and Remi with a future away from these mountains and away from that young man with the lovesick eyes. The kind of favor that would put you forever in my debt."

"Don't put yourself in debt or anything, but if you feel you must, go ahead. I know you, Winston. You'll call in your favors in whether or not I agree."

"At least I asked you first," Winston said. He pulled a pad of paper closer and made several notes to himself. A couple of phone calls to the right people would set up successful futures for them all. "I am brilliant," he murmured to himself.

Pushing himself out of his chair, Jeremy growled, "I'm going for a walk."

He stalked slowly across town and back, stopping at the Brass Rail only because his knee was protesting. Jeremy didn't want to go home yet. It was barely nine o'clock and there was nothing there except a Machiavellian choreographer who was more interested in his next production than Jeremy's concerns.

He didn't know why he felt like snarling at the world, but the black mood had descended fully over him. Remi wasn't a little girl any more. She was a young woman, and in a few short years, she'd be the same age her mother had been when she'd been born. The same age as when he'd had left town for Julliard, leaving behind his responsibilities.

"Sorry Jeremy, Chance is off tonight," Monique said. She sat a bottle of the imported beer he preferred in front of him.

"Of course he's off. He's never here when I need him," Jeremy muttered. He took a long draw from the beer. He finished the bottle before setting it down.

"You got keys tonight?" Monique asked. She opened another bottle and set it next to the first.

"No, I walked over," Jeremy said. He tried to smile, but the attempt fell flat. He just wasn't in a smiling mood.

He should be content. The production was coming along fine. The girls were astute. They were better than some professionals he'd worked with in the past. His relationship with Diane was going well, almost too well. The physical therapist was impressed with the progress he was making. The money Dottie left him was more than enough to see him through the next year or so, even if he didn't work again. Harry kept talking about lucrative opportunities during every one of their weekly telephone calls.

So why did he want to snap at the next person who looked at him?

22

Mr. Jeremy, what is the secret of the dance? The secret to making it as a professional dancer, I mean?" Marcie asked the question as she and Remi warmed up. It was the last rehearsal for the two girls alone before the dress rehearsals began the next afternoon.

They had so many questions about his life as a dancer and the dance world in general, and they'd come to an agreement. They were allowed to ask him any questions they wanted, but only while they stretched and warmed up. Once they began to dance, the questions stopped and the girls concentrated on their dancing.

Remi stretched and waited. She, too, wanted to know the secret, the key that would allow her to grow from a small town dancer into a world famous person like her uncle.

Jeremy straightened and looked at the two girls, his expression somber. "The secret of the dance is the same as the secret of anything, of life itself. You have to work hard and have passion. For dancing, for living, for whatever your interest may be."

The words struck a cord in Remi. It sounded like something Dottie would say. She studied her uncle closely. His eyes were sad, yet they also looked joyous, like he'd just discovered something. His eyes. They looked...they looked...then Dottie's words resounded in her memory. "I see your father in you, especially about the eyes."

"Oh my gosh," Remi breathed. Jeremy's eyes were the same as hers. He even had the three gold flecks of her brown eyes.

"What? Are you okay? You're not overdoing this, are you?" Jeremy asked, frowning in her direction.

"No, I'm great. I just figured something out," Remi said, "I think."

"Enough thinking of other things. You need to concentrate on the production. Now, to your places ladies. I want to run through this tonight without stopping unless we absolutely have to, okay?" Jeremy pushed to his feet and headed for the stereo.

"Yes, sir," the girls said as they rose. Remi took her place on one side of the room and Marcie sat on the piano bench, to wait until her entrance.

Was Jeremy her father? How could that be? If he was her father, why had he left her mother? Why did her mother marry her father?

Remi stumbled on her third step because her mind was drifting into the land of unanswerable questions. Taking a deep breath, she looked at her uncle. "Sorry, can we start again?"

Jeremy studied her and nodded. "Concentrate, but have fun. This is not supposed to be torture."

Remi nodded and listened to the music, then began her first pass across the stage again. She focused on the music and her movements, blocking out questions and wonders and guesses.

It wasn't until Jeremy was driving her home that her curiosity returned. Shifting in her seat, she studied her uncle. Now she could see there was more than just their eyes that were the same. Their mouths had the same curves as well.

The line of her jaw, though softened, had the same sharpness as her uncle's.

"What? Is my hair turning blue or something?" Jeremy asked after two minutes of having her silently study his profile.

"No, maybe a few silver strands, but not blue," Remi teased before turning to look out the front windshield again.

Silence descended once again while she tried to find the words to ask the question that could rock her world off of its solid foundation. Before she could formulate the most tactful phrasing of it, Jeremy pulled into her driveway.

"Thanks, Uncle Jeremy," Remi said as she grabbed her bag and climbed from the car, she was relieved that she could hold off a while longer on finding out who, exactly, was her father.

"I'll pick you up tomorrow after school for dress rehearsals," Jeremy said before putting the car in reverse and heading back to town.

$$\backsim$$

Jeremy's stomach began dancing the salsa as the cast and crew gathered for the first dress rehearsal of *The Cracked Nut*. The sets were in place, numbered, and the crew knew how and when to change them. The cast had provided their costumes as directed by Winston. Each costume had been checked and additions or changes made as necessary. Everything was ready for the first full cast run through. Almost.

Jeremy paced the aisle down the center of the auditorium, growling and muttering to himself. The only member of the cast he had yet to meet still had not made his appearance.

Though she was busy lining the girls up for their opening

number, Diane could see that Jeremy was going to start tearing down the stage if she didn't do something. She put Marcie in charge backstage and then headed toward the tense director. Walking up behind him, she touched his arm; she fought the urge to jump back when he spun around.

"Where is he?" Jeremy demanded. "Please tell me there is an actual flesh and blood form somewhere dressed in overalls and boots who knows Uncle's solo."

"Of course there's a man coming to dance the part of Uncle. Let me go and see if he's gotten held up by your stage door police."

Jeremy had enlisted the boyfriends of two of the older girls to guard the entrances that, per Mrs. Kelly's edict, remained unlocked. The boys' orders were to keep all spectators out so those involved in the production could concentrate. He needed the girls focused on the work at hand, not Mommy or Daddy in the audience.

Jeremy pushed through the door at the back of the auditorium, not surprised to feel resistance. Pushing harder, he called, "Step aside, Jim. I need to come out." The door opened easily as the young man shifted the chair he'd leaned against the door to sit in.

Stepping into the hallway, Jeremy looked around, studying the people sitting or standing in the lobby. He recognized most of them and nodded to those who gave him a smile or a wave.

He did not see a man in overalls and boots who looked like he should be onstage dancing. Turning to head back in and have words with his second-in-command, he paused when the door to the parking lot flew open. But it wasn't the dancer Diane had promised. It was Chance and Stacy.

Had they come to see the dress rehearsal? If so, they'd be

disappointed because Jeremy was only opening the last dress rehearsal to the public. This first full run through would be one of his last opportunities to have the girls to himself before nerves and stage fright could attack them. Hopefully, he'd prepared them sufficiently to ignore the audience.

A sigh escaped as he returned to the auditorium. Jim was putting his chair back into place when Chance strolled up. "Excuse me, I need to get in there," he said.

"Sorry, I can't let parents in today. The boss don't want nobody inside watching the rehearsal," Jim said. He examined the two who looked like parents to him. Mr. Applewhite had given him explicit instructions. He didn't want to disappoint the man who was giving Gwen, his girlfriend, a chance to live her dream of dancing onstage.

"I'm one of the dancers." Chance frowned at this hang up. They'd been late getting out of town because of an accident blocking Main Street in Romney.

"I guess it's okay if you're one of the dancers," Jim said. "Go on in," he opened the door and allowed the couple inside.

Chance stepped inside and pulled off the long trench coat. Stacy took his coat and settled into a seat in the back of the room. She was deep in the shadows and invisible from the stage.

"Diane, he's not here. How can we run a production when one of the featured dancers isn't here?" Jeremy groused as he stalked toward the stage.

"He's here," Diane responded.

"Sorry I'm late, but there was an accident on the mountain," Chance said. He aimed his apology toward Diane.

Jeremy swung around at the sound of the voice. "What are you doing here? I told Jim and Mark I did not want parents in here today."

"What are you talking about? I'm one of the dancers." Chance glanced from Jeremy, who looked as confused as he felt, to Diane who looked very pleased with herself.

"You're my Uncle?" Jeremy stuttered, putting the puzzle pieces together.

"No, dufus, I'm your brother. But I am dancing the part of Uncle in this production. You're the tight ass picky director?"

"So you've been with Diane all those times you were helping a friend?"

"Yep, and you were busy with the production when I couldn't get together with you," Chance laughed. "Somebody has pulled a real good 'gotcha' on us, wouldn't you say?"

"I'd definitely say," Jeremy said. "Well, I guess that takes care of whether or not you're cheating on your wife. Are you ready for rehearsal?" With a breath, he shifted into his role as director. A crowd of dancers had moved onstage to check out the two men laughing like lunatics, but Remi was strangely absent.

So she still hadn't told her father. The next minutes would be very interesting as a few more secrets were dragged into the light. "All right, ladies and gentlemen, let's get this show on the road!" He clapped his hands several times. The crowd dispersed, clearing the stage in seconds.

"I'll just go backstage and wait for my cue," Chance said as he headed for the three steps that led from the auditorium floor to the stage.

"Okay," Jeremy said. He was caught up in passing directions into his headset that connected him with Diane as well as the rest of the lighting and backstage crews.

Chance headed backstage. He wound his way through the girls who were waiting for their cue. Even though their costumes weren't traditional, he was able to identify all the featured performers except Clara.

Then he saw a young lady hiding behind the others, staring straight at him. From the top of her head she looked very familiar. Just like another young lady he knew who would give her eyeteeth to be in such a production.

"Remi?" He called out softly as he moved toward the form wearing a gingham dress and ballet slippers. There were so many people between them he had a hard time keeping sight of her. She ducked and disappeared.

He continued through the crowd, careful not to step on anyone's toes with his heavy boots. Why he had to have boots when trying to dance was beyond him. But the choreography called for boots. Thankfully there weren't a lot of jumps or other moves that called for flying.

The backstage area cleared when Diane called for those in the opening scene.

"Remi?" Chance found his daughter hiding behind a wooden tree that would be used later. "Honey, are you performing the part of Clara?"

"Hello, Daddy," Remi said. She took a deep breath and turned toward him. "What are you doing here? Did Uncle Jeremy tell you I was doing this? Or was it Winston?"

"Neither one, honey."

"Why are you here then? Jeremy doesn't like parents in the auditorium during rehearsals." Remi stepped out from her hiding place and took a good look at her father. "Why are you wearing that outfit?"

"I'm dancing the part of Uncle." Chance turned a circle, then bowed low. "What do you think? Do I look like an Uncle?" The irony of the question squeezed at his heart. He struggled to keep a smile on his lips.

Later, he'd have a long talk with his daughter about truth, honesty, and the American way. Right now he couldn't be mad. He was too proud of her. He was also nervous. He'd danced, sure, but never in front of people, except his students and they didn't count. What if Jeremy hated his interpretation?

"Remi? You're on in a minute, honey," Diane said as she appeared at Chance's shoulder with a worried look on her face.

Remi nodded and slipped past her father without another word. She was certain to hear about her deception later.

⌁

"All right, that's all for today. I'll see you here Tuesday for our first rehearsal in front of an audience. Don't change a thing you did today. Get here early so we can warm up," Jeremy called as the entire cast and crew gathered onstage three hours later.

Stacy approached from where she'd observed the entire rehearsal. She knew she wasn't supposed to be here, but she'd had to see for herself. This production would be a credit to her brother-in-law's reputation. Jeremy was a tough director, but she'd never seen a group look so professional.

"It was wonderful, Jeremy," she said touching his arm.

Jeremy turned to stare at her. "What are you doing in here?" he asked. His words were accusatory, but his smile sent a different message. "You're supposed to be outside waiting with the rest of those vulture stage mothers."

Stacy batted her eyes at him. "I snuck in and sat in the back row. They're very good." She nodded toward the girls who streamed past them on their way out.

"Mom! Guess what! Dad's dancing the part of Uncle.

And I'm Clara!" Remi threw herself into her mother's arms
as Chance approached slower, followed by Diane and Winston. Everyone looked pleased with the first dress rehearsal.

"So, who's buying dinner?" Winston asked in his inimi-
table British style.

"I think you should. You made more than God last year.
This one is going to be a hit as well, even if only in two small
towns." Jeremy shifted closer to Diane and wrapped one arm
around her shoulder to pull her close.

"Yes, but you're the one launching a new career once this
production closes," Winston predicted.

Jeremy stilled, but was not sure how to respond. Winston meant well, but what if the girls froze once there were
bodies in the seats? Diane squeezed his waist, but Jeremy
didn't acknowledge her. He was visualizing a future near the
stage, but never again in the center of the action. The vision
wasn't as distasteful as it had been in the past. Not as long as
he could work with the bright young talent of the future.

He stepped away from Diane. "I've got to get my bag.
I'll meet you in the parking lot." As he headed backstage, his
limp was more pronounced than it had been in quite a while.

"Oops," Winston murmured as he gathered his things,
then waited while the others did the same. "I didn't realize
the topic was still off-limits. He will have a brilliant career as
a director. All he has to do is admit that he's too old to return
to the stage."

Diane followed Jeremy backstage and found him staring
at his bag as if he'd never seen it before.

"He's right, you know. You're an incredible director. No
one could have done what you have in only six weeks. Not
without twice as many girls and three times as much rehearsal
time." Diane laid her hand on his shoulder and laid her cheek

against his upper arm. Every muscle was as hard as the granite that made up the nearby mountains.

"He's right. I'll never dance again." He gathered his bag and swung it over one shoulder. "Come on, let's go eat so much Winston has to get back to work to pay for the meal." Taking a deep breath, he tried to shake off the portent of doom that had descended over his shoulders during the last few minutes.

23

$\mathcal{J}$eremy scanned the article again.

THE FAMILY THAT DANCES TOGETHER

The Winchester Arts Council Christmas production has received high-powered assistance from the Applewhites of Romney, West Virginia. When Lynn Bowersox, who was supposed to direct this year, was injured in a car accident, world famous dancer Jeremy Applewhite stepped in to take her place. His brother, Chance, and niece, Remi, are to be featured dancers in this year's production called *The Cracked Nut*. Broadway choreographer Winston Christopher is responsible for this new updated version of the classic ballet, *The Nutcracker*. Performances are Friday and Saturday November 9th and 10th in Winchester and November 16th and 17th in Romney, West Virginia. Don't miss your chance to see this family production that will benefit the Winchester Arts Council and the Hampshire County Library. For more information, call the Arts Council at 555-0044.

A two-year-old publicity photo of Jeremy as well as a cover of the program accompanied the article. Jeremy hadn't known about the article until Sunday evening. In the space of an hour, three neighbors from up and down the block dropped by to leave him copies of the paper and get information about tickets for the Romney performances. In self-defense, Jeremy smiled devilishly and gave them Stacy's number. He could see her hand in this newspaper article.

"She's gone too far this time," he grumbled to Winston after Reverend Allbright and his wife dropped off yet another copy of the article.

"The Arts Council needs to sell tickets. Putting your name out there is guaranteed to pack the house." Winston looked up from the letter he'd been pouring over for the past hour. Mitchell had certainly grown long-winded. Or maybe Winston was just using it to avoid talking to him. He always did know when to avoid a fight and Jeremy was in the mood for a knock down, drag out.

"She should have warned me," Jeremy said as he paced the room like a caged tiger.

This was one of the few times he missed the big city. Small towns on Sunday night were not the time to want a drink and a diversion beyond G-rated television. He made a mental note to call first thing Monday to have cable hooked up.

"If she had told you, you would have only gotten angry," Winston said. He carefully folded his letter and returned it to its envelope. He'd read it again later, after he'd settled Jeremy down. "Why don't you go see Diane? She could take your mind off becoming a wildly successful director."

"She's got court tomorrow, and she's snowed under with work. I promised to stay away until Tuesday evening so she can try to catch up."

"Call Dr. Michaels and set up an appointment for to-morrow. It's time to have the knee looked at again. The future doesn't always take care of itself. Sometimes you have to help it along."

Jeremy threw himself into the rocker recliner. "Shut up, Winston. I don't want to think about the future for another month. My career is over and I don't know what else to do." Saying the words out loud was the hardest thing he'd ever done. It only made him feel more insecure.

"You can't do anything until Dr. Michaels figures out exactly what's wrong with that knee. Knowing the prognosis would make the future easier to face." Winston pulled the phone closer. Taking a business card off the bulletin board he'd set up next to the couch, he dialed the number on the back.

"Yes, I'd like Dr. Michaels to call me as soon as possible to set up an appointment for Mr. Jeremy Applewhite. The number is 307-555-5222. Thank you." Winston hung up the phone, crossed his arms and looked at Jeremy. "There, it's done. She said he'd be calling in for his messages in the next hour or so."

Jeremy jumped from his chair as if he'd been bit by a swarm of fire ants. "Why can't you leave well enough alone?"

"Because you're too talented to sit around this house for the next fifty years living on past successes. Putting this off just wastes time. The longer you're away from the stage, the harder it will be to make your comeback."

"Winston, there's no way I'll ever dance again. I'm too old and broken down. It's time to retire and move on."

"So do it. But first see Dr. Michaels and get through the next month. It's time to stop bitching and start dreaming again." Winston grabbed his letter and his briefcase and swept from the room.

✌

"I want to go in and have a look around," Dr. Michaels an- nounced Tuesday morning when Jeremy met him in his Man- hattan office. The doctor had examined the joint in ques- tion, ordered x-rays and an MRI, then compared them to the old ones from Jeremy's file.

"How soon?" Jeremy asked. He gritted his teeth against the new pain that began when the good doctor pushed his knee in, checking his range of motion.

"Monday morning. The procedure shouldn't take more than an hour or so, unless..." Dr. Michaels said. "I'm feeling something in there I don't like, but I can't see anything on these films."

"Can't we put it off for a month?" Jeremy asked. He had to be at the performances.

Some directors he'd dealt with would work with the dance troupe until the opening night, then slack off. They would either miss performances or spend the time they were sup- posed to be directing talking to people about their next project. Jeremy refused to be one of those directors. This was his pro- duction and by God, he was going to be there for each and every performance.

"No, it can't wait. If I had my choice, I'd slap you in the hospital today and do the procedure in the morning."

"I have a dress rehearsal tonight!"

"That's why I'm putting it off until Monday. The sooner I look at that knee, the better. If I don't do it soon, all we'll be able to do is replace the joint."

"All right then, Monday. Will I go home that day?"

"Yes, unless the problem is already beyond the repair stage. If that's the case, then I'm going to do whatever necessary to get you walking without that stiff-legged gait, even if that means replacing the joint."

Jeremy sighed. This man had been taking care of his legs for years and wouldn't threaten unless he had to. "All right, Monday morning. Now can I go? I have a dress rehearsal in a few hours and I need to get back." Pushing off the table, he grabbed the sweatpants he'd worn in and pulled them on.

"My nurse will call you Friday with all the information you need for Monday. Stay off that leg as much as possible between now and then. And bring your crutches with you to the hospital. No use having to buy a new set when you've already got a pair that works."

"Okay, okay. See you Monday." Jeremy slipped his feet into sneakers and hobbled out of the room as fast as he could.

❧

Jeremy hesitated in front of Diane's door, not wanting to use the key she'd given him. Something about letting himself into her apartment when she was home spoke of a deeper commitment than that of directing partners and three-time-a-week lovers. He'd left clothes here before and she'd even washed his underwear once, but this was different. Though he'd agreed to meet her here for an early dinner, using his key would imply he felt he could come and go as he pleased. That certainly wasn't the case. Instead, he repocketed the key and knocked.

"Come on in Jeremy, the door's open," came through the door.

Pushing it open, he stepped inside. "How did you know it was me?"

"I've been watching for you. You're late," she scolded.

"Sorry, the doctor's office was crazy," he said as he dropped his bag and crossed the room to pull her into his arms.

"Are you all right?" Diane returned his hug, then knelt and placed several kisses across the surface of his bad knee through his pants

"I'm fine, honey," Jeremy said. "But I'll be back on crutches Monday afternoon."

"Really? Why?" Diane asked.

"Dr. Michaels wants to take a look inside my knee to figure out what's wrong. The pictures he took don't show anything, but he felt something funny."

"I'll clear my schedule," Diane said.

"Yes, ma'am," Jeremy replied. Telling her not to come with him to New York would be like arguing with a wall. She was just as determined to have her way as he was to have his. "Let me change, then we can get to rehearsal."

"Do you want anything to eat?" Diane offered as he pulled off his shirt.

"I don't think I can eat. I'm too nervous," he said. He swallowed, hoping to return his stomach from his throat back to his abdomen. "But I'll take another kiss."

As long as he'd been dancing, as famous as he was, nerves always hit him on the firsts: First rehearsal, first dress rehearsal, and first performance. Once those were out of the way, he'd be fine. First nights were hell.

24

Tuesday evening, Jeremy paused outside the doors of the Arts Center to examine the scene before him. Copies of the newspaper article plastered the walls, next to the open auditorium doors, next to poster size copies of the program. There was a small group of people gathered just inside the front doors. One person carried a large video camera propped on his shoulder. Another wore an expensive 35-mm camera around his neck and a large camera bag over one shoulder. The other two carried small notebooks and seemed to be comparing notes as they waited.

"Uh-oh," he murmured, lifting his arm from around Diane's shoulder. "Looks like the vultures are circling." He spun around so they couldn't see his face. "You take care of them, honey, I'm going in the back door to the rehearsal room. Send the girls down there so we can warm up."

"Don't you want to talk to the reporters?"

"I hate talking to the press. I always say the wrong thing. You do it, okay?"

"I just hope I say the right things and don't get you in trouble." Diane watched the man she'd fallen in love begin to sweat.

"You'll do fine. Talk about the production, how hard the girls have worked, and what a good cause the Arts Council is. Just talk about the girls and their hard work."

Brushing a kiss across her cheek, Jeremy slipped around

the corner to the side entrance. He waved several girls who were coming in from the parking lot to follow him. He knew his instructions hadn't come out right, but he'd fix it later. Right now he had a production to get on stage. Diane would understand he wanted the press to focus on the girls and not on him, wouldn't she?

"All right ladies, are we ready to warm up?" He stripped off his sweatshirt and changed from his sneakers to the soft-soled dance shoes he wore during rehearsals. They allowed him to move around the auditorium silently.

"Mr. Jeremy, are we really ready to do this in front of people?" Marcie looked pale. She dropped her wool coat on her bag, then straightened the purple overalls she wore.

"You're going to be great. Now warm up those muscles!" He motioned the other girls into the room and began warming up.

～

Diane watched Jeremy disappear around the corner followed by several giggling mice. He was the Pied Piper leading them to their destiny. So he didn't want her to talk about him or their relationship. Didn't he think they had a relationship? Was he that unsure of her? Or of himself?

With a deep breath, she stepped inside, then crossed the lobby, breathing steady to calm the swarm of butterflies flying around her middle. "Hello, may I help you?" she addressed the clutch of people who came to attention at her approach.

"We'd like to speak with Mr. Applewhite," one of the reporters said.

"Mr. Applewhite has requested that he not be the focus of your interest. We'd like you to focus on the girls, the production, and the Arts Council," Diane replied. She tried to look apologetic and unwavering at the same time.

"Are the rumors that he'll never dance again true?" the other reporter asked.

"I'm afraid I can't say." Diane answered.

Before she could say anything else, Winston walked in with Stacy, Remi, and Chance. "If you'll excuse me, I need to get to work. Here's Mr. Christopher, the choreographer of our production. I'm sure he'll happy to answer your questions."

Diane waved Winston over. When he was right next to her, she turned around and whispered, "Say nothing about Jeremy."

Winston immediately turned on the charm that had been written about in magazines from *Vanity Fair* to *Dance World*. Diane listened long enough to hear him say, "Hello there, how is everyone today?" He'd obviously been handling reporters for a long time.

༼

Jeremy stood in the aisle as the curtains parted. The lights came up to show the inside of a barn. Only this barn was clean and had a decorated Christmas tree off to the left side. A moment later, the music began. The butterflies that had flitted around his stomach morphed into elephants that threatened to send him racing for the bathroom before the first dancer appeared. He scoffed at the idea of throwing up. He hadn't eaten since breakfast in preparation for just this moment.

"Take deep breaths. In through your nose and out through your mouth. Deep, slow breaths," Winston murmured.

"I am. It's not working," Jeremy replied. He knelt in the

aisle when a woman behind them hissed "Down in front."

When the dancers burst onstage Jeremy's nerves calmed. He became caught up in the dancing and the story. He lost track of the technical errors and the fact that two of the youngest girls were a half beat behind.

The music changed and the dancers shifted. The square dancers took center stage. Jeremy rose, backing up the aisle, always keeping his eyes on the stage. The dancers moved as he'd taught them, looking nervous but excited as they counted beats. None of them tried to find their parents in the handful of adults who'd come in to watch.

Through it all, he realized the hole in his soul that not performing had left behind was gone. He'd pulled this production off with next to nothing for a budget, time, or resources. What would he be able to do if he had the proper costumes, sets, and assistants?

ॐ

Three hours later, when the curtain closed for the last time and their audience of applauding parents rose to their feet, Jeremy knew where his future lay. Rising from the seat he'd taken in the last row, he slowly approached the stage. A group was waiting for him.

Behind the parents stood the reporters, wearing determined expressions. This time Jeremy knew they wouldn't be foisted off on anyone else. He would have to talk to them.

"Please don't let me screw this up," he murmured in a toneless whisper that hopefully only he and God could hear.

"Mr. Applewhite, you've done a wonderful job, even if your methods are rather unusual. When Caitlyn told me she was the Sugar Plum Fairy and not Clara, naturally we were disappointed. She thought you were showing favoritism to your niece, but I understand now. You've done a wonderful job," Caitlyn's mother said. She stepped closer, not waiting for Jeremy to join them. She was an older version of her daughter, more polished but just as image-conscious in her navy suit with shiny gold accessories.

"Thank you. The girls have worked very hard. I hope we'll have sold out performances," Jeremy said. He kept moving forward slowly, concentrating on minimizing his limp. He cut through the crowd, using the best advice someone had ever given him: when confronted with someone you don't want to talk to, smile, be polite, but keep moving. It makes them happy to talk to you for a few seconds and you get through the crowd and on your way with a minimum of fuss. He accepted kind words from the other parents who each had a compliment after criticizing his directorial technique.

"It's the results that count. I believe we have a winner here. I hope the rest of the community agrees with me." Leaving the stage parents behind, he had only the press gauntlet to run. Then he could go backstage and see his girls.

"Excellent production, Mr. Applewhite," the first reporter said. Her eyes offered an invitation for a one-on-one meeting, but Jeremy wasn't interested. The only lady he was interested in waited backstage.

"Thank you. I'm pleased with it," Jeremy said. He took another step, wanting only to get away. His ultimate goal was to get Diane alone.

"Rumor has it, you'll not be returning to the stage, that your knee has given out. Is that true?" The reporter backed up, keeping pace with him.

"Your rumor's wrong. I'm on vacation. Now, if you'll excuse me."

"A working vacation? Trying your hand at directing, just

in case?" The reporter refused to take the hint.

Jeremy gritted his teeth against a response that would burn a few ears and no doubt earn him a reprimand from both reporters and parents. "Excuse me, I need to see to my cast and crew."

The reporter continued to throw questions at his back, but he moved at a quicker pace, up the steps to the stage and then behind the curtain. What he found behind the heavy curtains could only be classified as chaos. Girls and adults were everywhere in little knots, giggling, squealing, and enjoying the post-show excitement. He remembered the feeling well. He scanned the crowd looking for Diane but couldn't find her.

Clapping his hands several times, he managed to lower the volume in the area. The girls crowded close with adults filling in behind them. They stared at him with anticipation, waiting for him to speak.

"You were terrific. There were only a couple of places where people got confused, but other than that, you did great! Now go home, eat dinner, do your homework, get a lot of rest, and be back here Friday evening at five." Jeremy smiled as he made the announcement.

"What about Thursday's dress rehearsal?" Marcie blurted out.

"We'll be fine without it. Don't forget to wash off the makeup before you leave."

Jeremy went on to answer several other questions as he made his way through the crowd. He commented to individuals on the minor errors they made and complimented those who'd performed flawlessly.

"You impressed me, brother," Jeremy said to Chance. "You should have been the one on Broadway, not me."

Chance didn't answer right away. Finally he said, "I don't think so. I was scared to death tonight, even knowing there were only a handful of people in the audience. I hope I don't embarrass us by freezing on Friday night." He pulled Stacy closer to his side, hugging her tight.

"You'll be fine. Just do the same thing you did tonight, and don't think about anything beyond the footlights. That's how I did it. You also might want to not eat before the performance. I'm always sick with nerves until I hit the stage."

"Me, too, Uncle Jeremy. But as soon as I'm done performing, I'm starving. Can we go eat now?" Remi studied her uncle and her father. They were so different, yet very much alike. And they both loved her, so did it really matter who'd donated the sperm and who'd raised her? They were family. Blood, love, and dance bound them together.

Someday soon, when she had time to think and had her mother alone, she would ask the question of who, exactly, was her biological father.

25

After monster burgers and fries on the way home, Remi entered the house just seconds before her parents. The answering machine was blinking. Pushing the play button, she grabbed the pen and pad that stayed by the phone. Anything to avoid homework.

Besides a page of math problems, she had to write an essay on what she wanted to do with her life and why. She wasn't sure she wanted to share her life's dream in an essay. She wasn't sure she could stand up in front of the entire class and say that she wanted to dance everywhere in the world there was a stage, just like her Uncle Jeremy.

"Uh, Remi, sorry I couldn't make the rehearsal today. Give me a call when you get this, okay? Oh, yeah, it's Toby. 555-6221." Click.

Remi wrote down the number, her smile growing. This was the first time he'd left a message for her. It must be important. She figured he was the one her dad had been complaining about. Someone had been calling, waiting for the answering machine to click on, and then hanging up without leaving a message.

As her father entered the kitchen, she hit the delete button. "Any messages?" Chance asked.

"Just one for me."

"You mean one of your friends finally left an actual message? That's incredible!" Chance chuckled. He bent over and laid his hands on the floor, stretching as many muscles as he could at one time. "I'm exhausted. I'm heading upstairs for a shower and bed."

"Night, Dad. You were great at rehearsal," Remi said. She pocketed the paper with Toby's number and picked up the portable phone.

Chance pulled her into a quick bear hug. "You were too, sweetheart. So beautiful. Even if you were kind of sneaky about getting the part."

"I'm not the only sneaky one in the family. I couldn't believe it was you when you said you were dancing the part of Uncle."

"Well, now the secrets are out," Chance said. He kissed her forehead, then released her. "Good night. Don't stay on the phone too long."

"Yes, sir. Sleep well."

Remi retreated to her room and waited until she heard the shower running upstairs. Only then did she call Toby. She paced the room, her stomach jumping around like her insides were on a trampoline.

The phone was answered on the second ring.

"Hello?"

"Hi, Toby!"

"Hi, Dancer. How did the rehearsal go?"

"It went really well. Uncle Jeremy didn't go to dinner with us because Diane disappeared. I think he did something to piss her off. She looked like she'd been crying."

"Uh-huh," Toby responded. He wasn't sure if she should be sharing this with him or not.

"Are you coming to the performance Friday night?"

"I got tickets for every performance, and I've switched shifts and called in favors to get the time off," Toby said.

He sounded proud of his accomplishment, but Remi immediately worried. "Are you sure you can take that much time off? You don't have to come to every show. I understand that work comes first."

"Just say 'thank you, Toby.' "

"Thank you Toby," she parroted.

"I was wondering if you'd wear my ring. I mean since we're going steady, I thought…"

"I'd love to," Remi cut him off.

"Can I give you a ride to school tomorrow? My mom's letting me drive the car."

"I'd like that a lot. Thanks."

"Okay, see you tomorrow."

"Bye."

"Bye, Dancer."

Remi hung up and did a quick jig in the middle of her bedroom. Toby wanted to give her a ring! She'd have to make sure he understood it wasn't an engagement ring or even an engaged-to-be-engaged ring. She didn't want to get his hopes up about their future, but it was so great to talk to him and spend time with him.

"Remi? Are you doing your homework?" her mom called.

"I'm starting it right now," Remi said. She tossed the phone on her bed, then sat at her desk and pulled out her notebook.

❧

"Marry me," Jeremy said softly. They'd left the others at the restaurant to spend time alone.

Diane's insides quivered at his words. "That wasn't a question."

Jeremy leaned over and took her lips. The kiss swept all thought from her mind. She wrapped her arms around him and returned his passion.

"Marry me," he repeated several minutes later when he finally released her lips.

"Yes," she whispered. Her mind and body had turned to mush, but that one word felt so right.

Jeremy pulled back and stared at her. "What did you say?"

"Yes," Diane repeated. Her smile grew.

"I know my future's kind of up in the air right now, but I am not going back to New York. My life there is over. But Harry has some rather bizarre offers of opportunities that he claims pay very well. And I have a few ideas of my own."

"Are you trying to convince me not to marry you now that I've said yes?" Diane asked. It didn't matter what he did for a living. Nothing mattered as long as he looked at her for the next fifty years just as he was right now.

"I just want you to know I don't plan on becoming a couch vegetable. I don't expect you to support us."

"That's good, because I have a few plans of my own. And they don't include you becoming a couch vegetable. Now can we quit talking about the future? I want to concentrate on the here and now," she said. She reached for the hem of his shirt and began to inch it up his chest.

"Do you have something specific in mind?" Jeremy asked. He helped her out of her own clothes as she pushed his out of her way.

"As a matter of fact, I do," she said. She leaned close to whisper the first of her ideas. It was a long time until morning and she didn't want to waste a minute

❧

Just after dawn, Chance stood outside the bathroom door. When he heard the toilet flush and water running, he knocked.

"Honey, are you okay?"

He counted to twenty, but she didn't answer. Fearful she'd fainted, he turned the knob and pushed the door open.

Stacy wasn't sprawled out across the tile floor unconscious. She was bent over the sink, her hair hiding her face.

"Stacy? You okay, honey?" he asked. He crossed to her side and laid one hand on her back.

"No, I'm not okay. I'm sick as a dog." Stacy lifted her head and met her husband's gaze in the mirror. "I just hope you and Remi don't get this."

Chance grinned like a fox. "I don't think we will. And if I remember right, you'll only have it for a few weeks. Just until your pants quit fitting."

With Remi she'd only been sick for a month. It had started the day after they'd been married; exactly two months after Jeremy had left town. It ended at three months, when suddenly she wanted to eat everything in sight. She never quite gained back the weight she'd lost, but Remi had been a healthy baby born exactly on her due date.

"What are you talking about?"

Chance pulled Stacy close. He wrapped both arms around her back. "I believe, my darling wife, that you have just suffered a bout of morning sickness."

"Morning sickness? You're crazy." Stacy rejected his insinuation.

"I remember a certain evening about two months ago where neither one of us gave a thought to anything except being together."

"Pregnant? But... How do you feel about this? I mean, we never talked about having a child together and..." Stacy began to cry, burying her head in his chest.

Chance hugged her tight, chuckling as she tried to burrow deeper. "I think it's fantastic. We're going to be parents

again. Another baby girl to spoil and teach the love of dance
to."

Stacy sighed deeply before lifting her head. "You know it
might just be a baby boy."

"Then I can teach him to love dance and sports," Chance
said. "Why don't you go back to bed. I'll get Remi off to
school. Then I'll call Dr. Yancey's office and see if he can fit
you in this morning."

"Sounds like a plan," Stacy said. She reached up and kissed
his chin before returning to the bedroom. "Maybe we should
keep this our secret for awhile. Just until we know for sure."

ॐ

Remi was dressed and ready for school long before a dark
green Ford Explorer pulled into the driveway.

"Bye, Dad."

"Have a good day, honey," Chance called from the kitchen.
He was brewing herbal tea for Stacy and buttering a cran-
berry muffin for himself.

Before he could make it to the front of the house, Remi
slipped out the door and danced across the lawn.

"Morning, Dancer." Toby put the truck in gear as soon as
she'd closed her door and fastened her seatbelt.

"Morning. How are you?"

"Not awake yet. Mornings should be outlawed," Toby
said. He drove with one eye on the winding mountain road
and the other on the young woman beside him.

She'd pulled her head back into a ponytail and wore faded,
skintight jeans and one of her father's burgundy sweatshirts
that advertised the restaurant. It was about three sizes too
big, but on her it looked elegant.

"Do you need a ride to town after school today?" he asked,

hoping for more time before making his simple offering.

"That'd be great. I have to see Uncle Jeremy after I check the mail for him." Remi settled in, her stomach quivery.

The rest of the drive was taken up with a discussion of the dance program and Toby's work. No mention was made of the ring.

Toby pulled into the parking lot and parked in the last row. He shut off the engine and pocketed the keys. "So," he began, unhooking his seatbelt and twisting in his seat. He reached into his shirt pocket, "it's not much, but I'd like you to wear this. If you want to, that is." He extended his hand across the space between the seats, the narrow band of glinting gold held between thumb and index fingers.

Remi looked at the ring for a long moment. "It looks really old," she said as she held out her right hand. Toby slipped the ring on her ring finger. It fit perfectly.

"It was my grandmother's. She was really little, like you. She called it a friendship ring and said I should give it to my best girl."

Remi held her hand and admired the ring. "It's beautiful, Toby. Thank you. I hope our friendship lives up to the beauty of this ring."

Toby leaned close, sliding one hand around the back of her neck. "I think it already has," he murmured. He closed the distance and kissed her.

Several minutes later, Remi pulled back. "We need to get going," she said, feeling lightheaded and breathless.

"Come on. I'll walk you to class."

As they walked toward the high school, Toby eased close enough for their arms to brush. Then he slid his hand around hers and, just like that, they were holding hands. A shiver raced up Remi's spine as his warm, callused palm brushed against her own.

"Can we keep this our secret for a while?" she asked.

"Sure. I'd rather not have your father questioning my intentions for at least another couple of years." Toby said as he pulled open the door to the school. "We'll just call it a friendship ring, okay?"

26

By the time the curtains parted on opening night, secrets were becoming harder and harder to keep. Everyone in the Applewhite family had news to share. Because they'd promised to keep the secrets, no one seemed to have anything to say.

Even Winston was unusually quiet as he oversaw the ticket collectors and ushers. When three familiar faces appeared in the crowd, he handed the programs he'd been passing out to the young woman beside him and slipped away.

"I'm so glad you could make it!" Winston exchanged hugs with each of the three men. "Come with me. I saved special seats for you." Pulling tickets from his pocket, he led the three into the auditorium.

"Do you want your name mentioned?" the tallest of the three asked as he settled into his seat. He pulled out a small notebook and a pen with a tip that glowed red.

Dance World magazine hadn't been interested in this small town production until Winston informed them that Jeremy Applewhite was directing. Then they wanted an exclusive story and interview with the reclusive man. Winston had been only too happy to cooperate with making arrangements for their reporter to get to town for opening night.

"Only if you have to, though I would like to see the faces

of those boobs who said this show wouldn't make it anywhere."
To the second man he said, "Clara is the young lady you need
to watch. She'd be a real asset to the school. I plan on talking
long and hard with her parents about her coming back to
New York with me, whether or not you offer her a place at
your school."

Leaning over he bussed the third man on the cheek. "Save
this seat for me, Mitchell. I'm so glad you made it back in
time. I'm sorry I didn't make your opening last month."

"I forgive you. I doubt the show will last the season. Besides, this sounds like it was a lot more fun." Mitchell squeezed
his friend's hand. "Does this count as your charity work for
the year?"

"Probably for the decade," Winston said. He returned the
hand squeeze and then went back to the lobby. He had to
make sure chaos hadn't broken out as it was prone to do on
opening night.

⌁

Two and a half hours later, the curtains closed to a standing
ovation.

Backstage, the dancers crowded around their director.
Jeremy opened his mouth to speak, but emotion overwhelmed
him. Nothing came to mind to express how proud he was of
his young dance troupe. Closing his mouth, he swallowed
hard, blinked back tears of joy and tried again.

"You did beautifully. I wouldn't change a thing. Now, wash
your faces and change your clothes. Make your parents take
you out for an ice cream to celebrate. Don't forget, we have
another show tomorrow."

The girls giggled as they dispersed, chattering about where
they should meet for their treat.

Jeremy found Diane directing the backstage crew. They were preparing the stage for the next evening's performance. As soon as she finished, he took her hand and led her to the janitor's closet. He pulled her into his arms before the door closed completely and lowered his head. She arched up to meet him halfway, her grin as big as his.

They'd barely begun to kiss when a knock interrupted. "What?" he growled between kissing Diane's lips and her jaw line.

"We're going to dinner and you're going with us, remember?" Chance growled back.

"Yeah, we're coming." Pulling back a half step, he cupped Diane's cheek in one hand. "One of these days I'm going to kill that brother of mine. His timing sucks."

"Not tonight. We have news and I think this would be the perfect time to share it." Diane returned his caress, the diamond and ruby ring on the fourth finger of her left hand glinting in the dim light.

"Are you sure? Once we make this announcement, there's no going back."

"Well, then I guess you'd better decide if you really want to marry me. I'm as certain as I can be. I love you, and that's all I need to know." Diane slipped from his arms and pushed the door open. "Give me five minutes to clean up."

Jeremy followed, his heart overflowing with her offhanded comment. He loved her and wanted to do what was right for them both. Frowning, he flipped off the closet light and let the door swing closed behind him.

"Hey brother, no frowning. You did a fantastic job with these girls. The Arts Council will be trying to get you to commit for next year before this show's even in the history books," Chance said.

Blinking, Jeremy focused on the man before him. "Well, they'll have to get in line. My dance school comes first."

"Your dance school? What dance school?" Chance trailed his brother through the backstage area.

"I'll tell you about it at dinner. Whether or not the surgery goes well on Monday, I'm going to be in Romney for a long, long time to come." He turned and grabbed his brother, pulling him in for a bear hug. "Thank you, Chance, for making the sacrifices so I could follow my dream." His words may have sounded cryptic to anyone overhearing them, but Chance understood them immediately.

"Thank you," he said before his throat shut down. "Stacy and I have a little announcement of our own."

"Oh, yeah? Well, give it up," Jeremy said. He released his brother, throwing one arm around him as they strolled toward the front door.

"Not yet. Secrets should be shared at just the right time."

"From the ring on her finger, I believe our little girl has a secret of her own to share. Who is he?" Jeremy couldn't help but notice the gold glinting on Remi's right hand as she danced.

"Toby North. He works at the restaurant. That's her secret to share, don't you think? There is he now. I didn't know he was going to be here tonight."

"Shall we grill him now or grill him later?" Jeremy asked. He waved the young man over as Winston approached from the other direction. Mitchell was beside him and two men followed. Winston had a grin on his face that said he had secrets of his own.

Studying the two strangers, he recognized the shorter bald one from the High School for the Performing Arts. He was rubbing his hands together like he'd found the next Isadora

Duncan. Was this Winston's surprise? Getting Remi into the high school of her dreams?

The taller man was a reporter, Mike something or other. Closing his eyes, Jeremy tried to remember where he worked. Was it *People* or *Dance World?* Maybe he'd give one of his rare-as-hen's-teeth interviews and leak his secrets. Not only was he off the bachelor market, he was also retiring from the stage and staying here in the mountains.

If he played it right, he could even promote the Applewhite School of Dance that he and Chance would be co-founding. Between them, with Diane and Stacy assisting, they could start a world class dance school. He would invite friends from New York to come and visit. They could study and even teach when they needed to get away from the city. Maybe granting an interview every now and again wouldn't be such a bad thing after all.

༈

During dinner, Remi remained silent as the adults around her shared their secrets.

Her mother was pregnant.

Uncle Jeremy would be having surgery on Monday in New York City, but would be returning to Romney to open a dance academy.

Uncle Jeremy and Miss Diane were engaged.

The news was surprising, but when Winston cleared his throat and looked her way, Remi's stomach clenched.

"One of the gentlemen in the audience this evening was a friend of mine. He is sort of a recruiter for the LaGuardia High School," Winston began.

The knot in her stomach grew larger and harder.

"He was very impressed with Remi and said to watch the

mail in the next week or so because there will be a letter offering you a space at the school for the January semester."

A month ago the news of the offer would have sent her out of her chair to dance around the restaurant. Now, though, her stomach flipped and she just stared at the messenger and felt tears fill her eyes. When she didn't answer right away, her father laid a hand on her shoulder.

"Remi, what do you say? Winston went to a lot of trouble to make your dream possible."

"Winston, thank you, but…"

"But what?" her mother asked when she didn't continue right away.

The knot that ballooned in her stomach clenched and Remi had to swallow hard before speaking. Taking a deep breath she looked at the small space across the table between Winston and his friend, Mitchell. "I don't want to go. I want to stay in town. I want to go to Uncle Jeremy's dance academy. Winston, you once told me that Uncle Jeremy could teach me more about the real world of dancing than anyone else. I want him to prepare me to take on the world." Remi blinked back sudden tears. "I'm sorry, Winston. I know you went to a lot of trouble to help my dream come true, but…"

"Dreams change," her father finished her sentiment.

"Yes, they do, thankfully," Jeremy added.

Winston's expression grew distracted. "My dear, I think you've made a very wise, mature decision. Whenever you're ready to come to New York, whether to go to school, to dance on the stage or just to visit, I'd better be your first phone call. I can just see your first starring role. Mitchell can produce, Jeremy can come to town and direct and I, of course, will do the choreography." His voice trailed off as he grabbed a paper napkin from the stack at his elbow and a pen from Mitchell's pocket.

"But it could be years before..." Remi protested.

"Forget it, Remi. When Winston gets like this, all you can do is ignore him until he returns to Earth," Jeremy explained as Winston continued writing and muttering to himself.

Twenty minutes later they left the restaurant. Winston was still creating, so Jeremy told the waitress to present him with the bill once he stopped writing.

Remi followed the adults and knew she'd made the right decision. As her father said, dreams change. But more so, she finally understood the secret of the dance. The dance of life was not much different than her passion to dance. And she wanted to enjoy them both, together. That was her new dream.